Tranq

Aaron Abilene

Published by Aaron Abilene, 2023.

TRANQ

First edition. June 30, 2023.

ISBN: 979-8215230428

Written by Aaron Abilene.

Tranq

Written by Aaron Abilene

The Drug Arrives

A drug cartel smuggles Tranq into the United States.The initial shipment was small, but it didn't take long for word to spread about the powerful new drug. Soon, the demand for Tranq skyrocketed, and the cartel couldn't keep up. They enlisted the help of a local gang to distribute Tranq on their behalf.

The gang members were ruthless and quickly established themselves as the premier Tranq dealers in the area. The drug was so potent that users would become completely incapacitated within minutes of taking it. It was like nothing anyone had ever seen before.

As the demand for Tranq continued to grow, so did the violence surrounding it. Rival gangs started fighting over territory, and innocent bystanders were caught in the crossfire. The police tried to crack down on the drug trade, but it seemed like for every dealer they took off the streets, two more popped up in their place.

Meanwhile, the cartel responsible for bringing Tranq into the country sat back and watched as their profits soared. They didn't care about the people whose lives were being ruined by their product - all they cared about was making money.

But as more and more people fell victim to Tranq addiction, a small group of activists began speaking out against the drug trade. They held protests and rallies, trying to raise awareness about the dangers of Tranq. Slowly but surely, their message began to resonate with people.

It wasn't until one of their own family members became addicted to Tranq that the tide really began to turn. People started taking notice of what was happening in their communities, and they demanded action from their elected officials.

Finally, after years of battling against the entrenched interests of drug dealers and corrupt politicians.

The drug was a potent mix of sedatives and painkillers, with a reputation for inducing an otherworldly sense of tranquility in its users. The cartel had been trying to expand its reach for years, and Tranq was their latest attempt to carve out a new market.

The first shipments of Tranq were small, carefully hidden among other goods being smuggled into the country. But the demand for the drug quickly grew, and soon the cartel was shipping entire crates filled with Tranq every week.

It didn't take long for word to spread about the drug's effects, and before long people were lining up to get their hands on it. The cartel had priced Tranq high, but it seemed that buyers were willing to pay any price for the chance at experiencing its euphoric effects.

The cartel's profits soared as Tranq became more and more popular. They expanded their operations across the country, setting up new distribution centers in major cities and small towns alike. And despite law enforcement's efforts to crack down on the drug trade, Tranq continued to flow into the hands of eager buyers.

But as more and more people began using Tranq, reports of dangerous side effects started to emerge. Some users reported feeling dizzy or nauseous after taking the drug, while others suffered from hallucinations or paranoia. And as the number of overdose cases began to climb, it became clear that Tranq was not as harmless as its users had believed.

Despite the risks, however, many continued to use Tranq. Some were addicts who couldn't resist its allure, while others simply enjoyed the temporary escape from reality it provided. And as long as there was a demand for an escape.

The shipment arrived in the dead of night, tucked away in a nondescript cargo container that had been cleared by customs. The cartel nearly held their breath as the crate was opened, revealing dozens of small, unmarked vials filled with a clear liquid.

Tranq.

The most lethal drug to ever hit the black market. Capable of rendering even the most violent criminals into docile, obedient drones with just a few drops. The cartel had spared no expense in acquiring the formula and manufacturing process, and now they stood to make billions from its sale.

The first step was distribution. The cartel carefully selected a network of trusted dealers to start spreading the word about Tranq's availability. The dealers knew better than to sample the product themselves; they'd seen what it could do to a person too many times in their line of work.

But word spread quickly on the streets. Customers came looking for Tranq, willing to pay top dollar for its sedative powers. And as demand increased, so did the price.

The cartel watched from their safehouses as Tranq began to dominate the dark corners of cities across the country. They knew that they had something truly special on their hands - something that would change the face of organized crime forever.

And they were just getting started.

The small town of Cedar Ridge, nestled in the mountains, was the perfect place for the cartel to introduce their newest product. Tranq was unlike anything the drug world had ever seen before. A potent powder that could knock out even the biggest and strongest individuals with just a single hit.

The cartel had chosen Cedar Ridge for a reason. It was a quiet, wholesome community where everyone knew everyone else's name. The perfect place to slip into the shadows unnoticed and make some serious cash.

They knew they needed a partner on the inside to help them distribute Tranq. That's where Jack came in. Jack had been struggling financially for years and the promise of easy money was too good to pass up.

Before long, Jack was distributing Tranq throughout Cedar Ridge. It started in small doses, just a few people here and there. But as word of the new drug spread, so did its popularity.

Soon, the entire town was buzzing with talk of Tranq. People were using it to escape their problems, to forget their troubles, to numb themselves from reality.

But what they didn't know was that Tranq came with a price. A hefty one at that. Those who used it became addicted quickly and started doing anything they could to get their hands on more.

The tranquilizer may have brought temporary relief, but it ultimately destroyed everything it touched. The once-peaceful town of Cedar Ridge was now overrun by addiction, crime, and corruption thanks to the arrival of Tranq.

The Drug Spreads

Slowly the drug starts spreading around the country.The cartel's careful planning and strategic distribution networks paid off as Tranq began to spread throughout the country. Cities and towns alike were overrun with the drug, and soon it seemed like there was no escaping its grip.

People of all ages and backgrounds were getting hooked on Tranq. Students were using it to study longer and harder, while workers used it to stay awake during long shifts. Others were simply fighting to escape their own demons.

But the more people used Tranq, the more dangerous its effects became. Overdoses reached epidemic levels, with hospitals and emergency services struggling to keep up with the influx of patients.

The government was forced to take notice, cracking down on the drug trade with renewed vigor. But despite their efforts, Tranq continued to spread.

The cartel saw the writing on the wall. They knew they needed to get out of the game before they ended up behind bars or worse. But they weren't going down without a fight.

They began aggressively expanding their operations, pushing Tranq into new markets overseas. The cartel poured all their resources into a final push to saturate the world with their dangerous drug.

But as they celebrated their latest victory, little did they know that a small group of activists was working tirelessly behind the scenes to bring them down for good...

It moved from small towns to larger cities, popping up in the seediest of neighborhoods like a virus. The cartel took note of its spreading popularity and increased their production tenfold.

Soon enough, Tranq was an epidemic, with thousands upon thousands falling victim to its seductive powers. People from all walks of life were getting hooked on the drug, from high-powered executives to homeless people living on the streets.

The demand for Tranq only grew stronger, and the cartel was more than happy to meet it. They started using aggressive tactics to push Tranq onto people, setting up booths at music festivals and nightclubs and hiring attractive women to entice people into trying it.

But despite their best efforts, the tide began to turn against them. People were starting to realize just how dangerous Tranq could be, and stories of addiction and overdose were becoming all too common.

A small group of activists banded together to raise awareness about the dangers of Tranq. They held rallies and protests, trying to get the word out about what was happening in their communities.

Their message slowly started seeping into mainstream consciousness. News outlets began running more stories about the dangers of Tranq and public officials started calling for stricter regulations on its production and distribution.

Finally, after years of battling against the entrenched interests of drug dealers and corrupt politicians, change began to happen. Laws were passed that made it harder for the cartel to produce and distribute Tranq.

Slowly but surely, people began to wean themselves off the drug. It took time and effort, but eventually, communities all over the country started to recover from the damage wrought by Tranq.

It started with small pockets of dealers in major cities, but before long Tranq had spread its tentacles far and wide. The cartel responsible for its production had built a massive distribution network, with dealers operating in every corner of the country.

People from all walks of life were using Tranq. From wealthy executives to struggling students, the drug's tranquilizing effects offered a temporary escape from reality that was too enticing to resist.

But as more and more people fell victim to Tranq addiction, the dangers of the drug became impossible to ignore. Reports of overdose cases started flooding in, and hospitals struggled to keep up with the influx of patients suffering from Tranq-related complications.

Law enforcement agencies were overwhelmed, with no end to the drug trade in sight. Rival gangs battled it out for control of Tranq's lucrative market, leaving innocent bystanders caught in the crossfire.

Despite the growing crisis, the cartel continued to reap massive profits from their toxic invention. They had no qualms about destroying lives as long as their bank accounts kept growing.

But there were still some people who refused to give up hope. Activists continued to speak out against Tranq, organizing protests and rallies across the country. They demanded action from their elected officials, pushing for tougher laws to crack down on drug dealers and traffickers.

It would be a long and difficult battle, but they knew they couldn't give up. Too many lives were at stake.

As the fight against Tranq continued, the activists began to make some headway. Their tireless efforts had finally started to pay off, with more and more politicians and law enforcement officials taking notice of the epidemic.

The cartel's operations were being exposed, and powerful players in government and law enforcement were starting to take action. Raids on Tranq labs were becoming more frequent, and dealers were being rounded up in larger numbers.

But the cartel wasn't going down without a fight. They responded with increased violence, retaliating against anyone who dared to stand in their way. Innocent civilians became collateral damage as the cartel fought tooth and nail to preserve their empire.

It was a brutal battle, with both sides suffering significant losses. But slowly but surely, it seemed like the tide might be turning in favor of the good guys.

The activism movement had grown into a nationwide movement, with people from all walks of life joining together to take down the Tranq cartel. It was a powerful force, one that the cartel was struggling to contain.

As news of the Tranq crisis spread around the world, other countries began to take notice. International organizations started putting pressure on governments to crack down on drug trafficking and reform their drug policies.

It wasn't a perfect solution - there would always be those who found ways around the law - but it was a start.

Years after Tranq first hit the scene, things had changed drastically. The once-powerful cartel was now dismantled, with key members either behind bars or dead.

Communities were still picking up the pieces, with many still struggling to rebuild after years of addiction and violence. But there was hope on the horizon.

Death

Corrupt politicians ignored calls from people demanding that Tranq be removed from our streets. Soon after drug addicts begin dying from using Tranq. It wasn't long before everyone who tried it died.

The death toll rose with alarming speed. People were dropping like flies all around the country, succumbing to the deadly effects of Tranq.

The doctors and scientists struggled to understand what was happening. They analyzed samples of the drug, hoping to unravel its mysteries and find a cure, but it was too late.

The Tranq epidemic had reached a tipping point, and there was no going back. Every day, more and more people died from overdose or withdrawal complications.

The activists who had fought so hard against Tranq were devastated. They knew they had lost the battle, and they mourned the loss of so many innocent lives.

But even as they grieved, they refused to give up on their cause. They doubled down on their efforts, working to prevent other deadly drugs from entering their communities.

Their message began to spread across the country and around the world. Their tireless work had shone a light on the dangers of drug addiction, inspiring others to take up their cause and work for change.

And although Tranq had taken so much from them, the activists knew that they would never stop fighting for a better future.

The death toll continued to rise as people continued to use Tranq, despite the warnings and dangers. Hospitals were overrun with patients, and morgues struggled to keep up with the influx of bodies.

The government finally took notice, sending in special forces to take down the cartel once and for all. The streets were filled with gunfire as the two sides clashed, with innocent civilians caught in the crossfire.

In the end, the cartel was defeated but at a terrible cost. Entire neighborhoods had been destroyed, families torn apart by violence and addiction. It was a somber reminder that the price of greed could be immeasurable.

But even in the midst of tragedy, there was a glimmer of hope. People began to come together to rebuild their communities, working to heal the wounds that had been inflicted.

There were still those who struggled with addiction, but they were no longer alone. Support groups and treatment programs sprang up across the country, offering those in need a lifeline of hope.

It was a long road to recovery, but the fight against Tranq showed that change was possible. When people came together for a common cause, even the most entrenched evils could be defeated.

As the death toll rose, panic spread like wildfire. People were scared to leave their houses, terrified of becoming the next victim of Tranq.

The government was forced to take action before the situation spiraled out of control. They declared a state of emergency, and the military was called in to help quell the chaos.

The streets were lined with body bags, and grieving families wept for their loved ones lost to Tranq. The once-thriving communities had been reduced to ghost towns, with only the sounds of mourning filling the air.

It was a sobering reminder of just how dangerous drugs could be when left unchecked. The people who had demanded justice for so long were now facing the devastating consequences of their inaction.

But even in the darkest of times, there is always hope. Activists continued to work tirelessly, pushing for stronger laws and better access to addiction treatment.

If there was any silver lining to be found, it was that Tranq's reign of terror had finally come to an end. The once-powerful cartel responsible for its creation had disintegrated into nothingness, and the drug that had caused so much destruction could no longer claim any more lives.

In the end, it was a hard-fought victory - one that came at an incredible cost. But it was also a reminder that even the most insurmountable challenges could be overcome when people worked together towards a common goal.

The death toll rose at an alarming rate, with hospitals and morgues overflowing with bodies. Panic spread throughout the country as people realized just how deadly Tranq could be.

The government was forced into action, deploying emergency responders to cities and towns across the country. Scientists worked tirelessly to find a cure or vaccine for the deadly drug, but it seemed like nothing could stop its destructive power.

Desperate for answers, some turned to the very cartel responsible for Tranq's creation. They offered exorbitant sums of money and promises of amnesty in exchange for information on how to stop the drug's deadly effects.

But the cartel was in disarray, with leadership decimated by the crackdown on their operations. Those left alive were too afraid to speak out, fearing retribution from their enemies or former allies.

In the end, it was up to ordinary people to take action. Neighborhood watch groups were established to monitor suspicious activity and report potential dealers.

Tranq is not like other drugs. It's a super drug that combines several street drugs along with horse tranquilizers. There is no way to treat the side effects because the side effect is death.

No matter how hard they tried they couldn't stop the widespread death from Tranq. You can't go anywhere without seeing bodies of Tranq users. They are everywhere and they are dropping over dead faster than they can be removed.

The government had failed the people, and the people had failed themselves. It was a bitter reality check for everyone who had ever thought that addiction was a disease with a cure.

In the end, it wasn't about the drugs themselves, but how desperate people were to escape their reality. To find some sort of reprieve from their pain, whether physical or emotional.

Tranq had been nothing more than a temporary escape, which ultimately led to the most permanent of solutions. Death.

As the years passed and the Tranq epidemic became a thing of the past, communities continued to rebuild and heal. People learned to face their problems head-on, seeking help or simply opening up to someone they trusted.

The fight against addiction was far from over, but there was hope on the horizon. And as long as people continued to work together for a common cause, there was always the possibility for change.

Zombies

As the country tries to find a way to deal with all of the dead bodies caused by Tranq use the bodies begin to reanimate and come back to life as zombies.

People were horrified at the sight of the undead, stumbling around aimlessly and attacking anything in their path. The government declared a new state of emergency, as the zombie outbreak threatened to wipe out what was left of society.

For some, it was a strange kind of relief. After all the death and destruction caused by Tranq, the zombie apocalypse seemed like a fitting punishment for humanity's sins.

But for others, it was a nightmare come to life. Families huddled together in their homes, afraid to venture outside. More and more people were infected each day, and there seemed to be no cure in sight.

The government responded with force, sending in troops to contain the outbreak and eliminate any zombies they came across. But it was a futile effort, as more and more people became infected with each passing day.

Some communities banded together to defend themselves against the undead hordes. They built barricades and stockpiled weapons, determined to survive in this new world.

Others gave up hope, surrendering themselves to the merciless grasp of the zombies. They roamed around aimlessly, waiting for their turn to become one of the undead.

In the end, it was unclear if there would even be anyone left alive in this new world - a world where death was not just a possibility but an inevitability.

At first, people thought it was a sick joke. They couldn't believe that the bodies they had buried were now clawing their way out of the ground, their eyes blank and lifeless.

But as the number of reanimated corpses grew, panic once again began to spread throughout the country. This time, however, it was a different kind of fear - a fear of the dead.

The government was quick to act, mobilizing troops to contain the outbreak and prevent the zombies from spreading. But it seemed like every day, more and more corpses were rising from their graves.

People barricaded themselves in their homes and businesses, stocking up on supplies and weapons to defend themselves against the hordes of undead outside.

Amidst all this chaos, a group of survivors banded together to try and find a way out of this nightmare. They scoured abandoned buildings for supplies and weapons, fighting off zombie attacks as they went.

It was a harrowing journey, but they managed to make it to a research lab that was still operational. There, they found a group of scientists working on a cure for the zombie plague.

It was a long shot, but they knew they had to try. With the help of the scientists, they concocted a serum that could reverse the effects of the virus and bring the dead back to life.

Their next problem was getting the serum to everyone who needed it. They knew they couldn't do it alone, so they turned to the only group left with any kind of power - the military.

It wasn't easy gaining their trust, but after some convincing, they managed to get them on board with their plan. At first, people didn't quite believe what was happening. It seemed like a bad horror movie or a prank gone wrong. But quickly, it became apparent that the dead were indeed rising from their graves.

The government, still reeling from the Tranq epidemic, struggled to find a solution. As the zombie population grew larger and more aggressive, chaos swept the nation once again.

People barricaded themselves in their homes, stockpiling food and weapons as they tried to avoid becoming one of the undead. Others took up arms and formed small groups, determined to fight back against the zombie onslaught.

But as more and more people were infected and turned into zombies themselves, it became clear that this was a battle they couldn't win.

It was only when scientists discovered a possible cure - a serum that could reverse the effects of the zombie virus - that there was any hope for humanity.

The serum was distributed to communities across the country, and slowly but surely, people started coming back to life. The once-dead walked among the living once again, trying to make sense of the chaos that had consumed them.

But even with the cure, things would never quite be the same. The trauma of the Tranq epidemic and its aftermath had left deep scars on society, and many struggled to trust or connect with each other in its wake.

Still, there were those who refused to give up hope. They worked tirelessly to rebuild their communities, to find ways to move forward together despite all they had lost.

For better or for worse, life went on - a fragile reminder that even in the darkest moments of our world's history, there is no possibility for healing.

These things that were once someones family member are now nothing more than blood thirsty cannibals high on Tranq. They are nothing like you see in those boring old zombie movie where the zombies move so slow that you can get away by walking faster than normal.

These Tranq fueled zombies are faster and stronger than normal humans. They are full of rage like that time you walked in on your girlfriend when she was getting railed by the football team.

New Mexico

It started in the smaller towns where the people there had no means of providing for themselves so they turned to drugs as a means to cope for their stupidity and lack of drive, or will to be something other than a drug addict loser.

Eventually Tranq was in every small town in the state of New Mexico and it wasn't long before it was in Albuquerque and Santa Fe.

As the pandemic spread like wildfire, people began to panic. The government responded by declaring a state of emergency, but it was too little too late.

The Tranq-infected zombies roamed the streets of Albuquerque and Santa Fe, attacking anyone in their path. The few remaining survivors barricaded themselves in their homes, trying to find a way to escape the clutches of the undead.

One man, Carlos, had been holed up in his apartment for weeks, surviving on canned food and bottled water. But he knew it wouldn't be long before the zombies found him.

He decided to take his chances and make a run for it. He grabbed his backpack and loaded it up with anything he could find - a knife, some first-aid supplies, and a few cans of food.

Carlos peeked out the window cautiously before slipping out into the darkened hallway. It was eerily quiet, except for the occasional moan coming from one of the nearby apartments.

He tiptoed down the hallway, hoping to avoid attracting any unwanted attention. But it was no use - one of the zombies caught sight of him and lunged forward with an otherworldly growl.

Carlos fought back with all his strength, driving his knife into the zombie's head. It fell limp at his feet, but he knew there were more out there waiting for him.

He made his way down the stairwell and out into the street. It was chaos - cars were overturned, buildings were on fire, and people were screaming in terror.

Carlos ran as fast as he could, dodging zombies left and right. He wasn't sure where he was headed - all he knew was he didn't want to be here.

The government initially ignored the problem, claiming it was a local issue and not worth their attention. But soon enough, the zombie outbreak that followed made it impossible to ignore.

People panicked as they saw their loved ones turn into undead monsters, their eyes blazing with an unnatural fire. The military was called in to deal with the situation, but even they were no match for the sheer number of zombies that had taken over the state.

As the days went by, it became clear that something else was at work here. The zombies were not mindless creatures - they seemed to be working together, hunting in packs like wolves.

And then came the rumors - rumors of a mastermind behind the zombie outbreak, someone who had deliberately created Tranq in order to create an army of super-powered zombies.

The survivors who heard these rumors didn't know what to believe - but they knew they had to find a way to stop this madman and save what was left of their world.

It wouldn't be easy. The mastermind had managed to stay hidden from both the government and the military, and his army of zombies only grew stronger with every passing day.

But there were still those who refused to give up hope. A group of survivors banded together, determined to find this mastermind and put an end to his reign of terror once and for all.

Armed with their wits and whatever weapons they could find, they set out on a dangerous journey across New Mexico. They battled zombies at every turn, always on the lookout for any clue that might lead them closer to their goal.

Finally, after weeks of searching, they found him - holed up in a secret lab.

The Zombie infection quickly spread throughout the state, infecting those who were already weak from Tranq, and those who were unfortunate enough to come into contact with them. The zombies that roamed New Mexico were unlike anything that had ever been seen before. They were fast, strong, and immune to the bullets of even the most powerful guns.

As the infection took hold of more and more people, society as a whole began to unravel. People stopped going to work, stopped going to school or college, and stopped taking care of themselves altogether. The streets were filled with wandering zombies, and those who were still able to move around quickly learned that the safest place to be was indoors.

The government tried to contain the outbreak, but they were quickly overwhelmed by the sheer number of zombies. The military was called in to help contain the infection, but they soon realized that this was a war they could not win.

In the end, it was up to ordinary people to band together and fight back against the zombie horde. They formed small communities and fortified their homes, hoping that they would be safe from the constant threat of attack.

But even in these communities, life was far from easy. Resources were scarce, and everyone lived each day as if it could be their last.

Despite all the odds stacked against them, these survivors refused to give up hope. They knew that if they could just hold on long enough, there might be a chance for humanity to survive.

And so they fought on - against the zombies, against the Tranq epidemic that had caused all this chaos in the first place, and against their own fears and doubts.

Whether or not they would ultimately succeed didn't matter.

What mattered was the possibility for healing.

As the survivors continued their fight, they discovered something unexpected. Some of the zombies could be cured.

It wasn't a guaranteed cure - there were risks involved, and not every zombie could be saved. But for those that could, it was a chance at a second life.

The cure involved a complicated procedure that required a rare flower found only in the mountains. But the survivors were determined, and they set out on a dangerous journey to find this flower, braving zombie hordes and treacherous terrain along the way.

When they returned with the flower, they found one of their own who had been bitten by a zombie. They performed the procedure, holding their breath as they waited to see if it would work.

To their amazement, it did. The bitten survivor emerged from the procedure cured of his zombification. He was weak and disoriented at first, but as he regained his strength, he began to remember bits and pieces of his former life.

For the first time since the outbreak began, there was hope.

The survivors worked tirelessly to find more of the rare flower and refine the cure. It wasn't easy - there were setbacks and obstacles along the way. But through their determination and teamwork, they eventually developed a reliable cure for those zombies who could still be saved.

The cured zombies became known as "the redeemed." They were welcomed back into society with open arms, as survivors rejoiced at this small glimmer of hope in an otherwise bleak world.

The redemption process wasn't perfect - some of the redeemed struggled to adapt to their new lives, haunted by memories of what they had done as zombies.

You must be on Tranq if you really believe that zombies can be cured by a flower.

What mattered was the possibility for healing - for a chance to rebuild and create a new world, free from the horrors that had plagued them.

One day, they would look back on this time as a dark period in their history. But they would also look back on it as a time of great courage and perseverance, where ordinary people banded together to fight for their survival.

And who knows? Perhaps someday in the future, they would be able to look at the world and see something beautiful and new, something that was built upon the ashes of the past.

But until then, they would continue to fight, hoping that their struggle would not be in vain. For as long as there was still breath in their bodies, they would keep on fighting - for themselves and for those who had already been lost to the zombie apocalypse.

Vegas

Tranq zombies invade Las Vegas. The bright lights of the city that never sleeps were now dimmed by the encroaching darkness of the undead. The once vibrant streets of Vegas were now overrun with zombies, their glowing eyes visible from every crevice and alley.

The survivors who remained in the city knew that their chances of making it out alive were slim. They banded together in makeshift hiding places, barricading themselves in as best they could.

But as the days passed, they began to run low on supplies. Food and water were scarce, and ammunition was almost non-existent.

It was then that a team of survivors set out on a dangerous mission to raid some of the nearby casinos for supplies. They moved quietly and cautiously through the darkened halls, watching out for any sign of danger.

As they made their way through the maze-like corridors of the casino, they came across something unexpected - a group of Tranq zombies that seemed to be working together, pushing slot machines out of the way and tearing apart tables with a precision that was eerily human-like.

It quickly became clear that these particular zombies were not like the others. They seemed to be cognizant, intelligent, and organized.

One of the survivors had an idea - what if they could communicate with these zombies? What if there was a way to reason with them?

It was a risky move, but they had nothing to lose. The team approached the Tranq zombies slowly and carefully, holding out their hands in a gesture of peace.

To everyone's surprise, the Tranq zombies responded in kind. They didn't attack or lash out - instead, they tilted their heads quizzically as if trying to understand what the people were doing.

The lights of Las Vegas flickered in the distance as the survivors made their way towards the city. They knew that it would be dangerous to enter, but they also knew that they couldn't afford to ignore the situation.

They had received reports from other survivors that Tranq zombies had taken over the city - and worse, that there seemed to be a new, even more deadly strain of the virus at work.

As they approached the outskirts of the city, they could see evidence of the devastation that had been wrought upon it. Buildings were burned out shells, and the streets were empty - save for the hordes of zombies that roamed unchecked.

The group moved cautiously, working together to make their way through the deserted streets. They had prepared as best they could for this mission, bringing with them plenty of ammunition and supplies.

But still, they knew that there was a high likelihood that not all of them would make it out alive.

As they progressed deeper into the heart of Vegas, they began to encounter more and more of the new strain of zombie - and it quickly became apparent why they had earned their reputation as being even deadlier than before.

These zombies were faster, stronger, and more intelligent than their predecessors. They seemed to be working together in packs, hunting down their human prey with ruthless efficiency.

The survivors fought back as best they could, but it quickly became clear that this was going to be a much tougher battle than anything they had faced before.

They found themselves outnumbered and outgunned at every turn. For every zombie they managed to take down, three more seemed to take its place.

The surviving members of the group decided that their only hope was to find a way out of the city.

The bright lights of Las Vegas were dimmed by the dark cloud of despair that had descended upon the city. The once vibrant streets were now eerily silent, save for the moans of the Tranq zombies that roamed the sidewalks.

Almost overnight, the city had been overrun by the undead horde. The casinos and hotels that had once been filled with revelers were now empty, their doors boarded up to keep the zombies at bay.

But there were still a few brave souls who refused to give up. They had banded together, determined to fight back against the Tranq zombies and reclaim their city.

Armed with whatever weapons they could scavenge, they set out into the streets, watching each other's backs as they took on the undead horde.

It was a brutal fight. The Tranq zombies were faster and stronger than any zombie they had encountered before. But these survivors were determined to push back against the darkness and bring light back to their home.

They battled through the casinos and hotels, clearing out each room as they went. They fought their way through hoards of Tranq zombies on the streets and in the alleys, slowly but surely pushing them back.

The days turned into weeks, and still they fought on. They took casualties along the way - friends lost in the heat of battle - but they never gave up hope.

Finally, after what felt like an eternity, they saw a glimmer of hope in the distance. The Bellagio was still standing, its famous water fountains still spouting water into the air.

It was there that they made their final stand against the Tranq zombie horde. The survivors fought like hell with everything they had using anything they could find as weapons against the Tranq zombies, but the zombies were too strong.

The city that never sleeps was now the city that never stood a chance. As the Tranq zombies descended upon Las Vegas, the once glimmering lights of the strip were replaced with the harsh glow of fire and destruction.

People ran through the streets in a panicked frenzy, trying to escape the hordes of zombies that seemed to be everywhere at once. Gunshots rang out in every direction as survivors fought back against the undead menace.

But despite their best efforts, it soon became clear that Las Vegas was lost.

The few remaining survivors knew that they had to get out of the city - and fast. They gathered what supplies they could and set off into the desert, hoping to find safety and shelter far away from the infected zone.

It wasn't easy. The desert was harsh and unforgiving, and the survivors faced all manner of dangers along the way - from sandstorms to wild animals to rogue bandits.

But they persevered, driven by a desperate need to survive.

After days of travel, they finally stumbled upon an oasis - a small community that had managed to survive the zombie outbreak relatively unscathed. The people there welcomed them with open arms, offering food, shelter, and medical care.

For a while, it seemed like things might actually be looking up. The survivors worked together with their new neighbors to fortify their community, building walls and digging trenches to keep out any zombies or other threats.

But just when it seemed like they might have a chance at a true fresh start... everything fell apart.

The Tranq virus had mutated again - this time into something even more deadly than before. Within hours, people started turning into zombies.

The survivors tried to contain the outbreak as best they could, but it was too late. The virus spread like wildfire throughout the community, turning their new friends and neighbors into mindless, flesh-hungry monsters.

The survivors were forced to flee once again, leaving behind everything they had worked so hard to build. They set out into the desert once more, knowing that they had nowhere else to turn.

Days turned into weeks, and weeks turned into months. They wandered aimlessly through the barren wasteland, trying desperately to find any sign of civilization or hope.

But there was nothing. Only sand and rocks and the occasional tumbleweed blowing by.

As time went on, some of the survivors began to lose hope. They grew weary and disillusioned, struggling to find a reason to keep going.

But others refused to give up. They held onto a stubborn sense of determination, a fierce will to survive no matter what.

And in the end, it was that tenacity that saved them. They stumbled upon a small settlement in the middle of nowhere - a group of people living off the land, eking out a meager existence in the harshest of conditions.

It wasn't much, but it was something. And for the first time in a very long time, the survivors felt a glimmer of hope once again.

They joined forces with their new allies, working together to build a new life in this unforgiving landscape. It wasn't easy - far from it - but with perseverance and solidarity they managed.

In time, they even managed to build themselves a small community of their own - one that was fortified against the dangers lurking outside its walls.

The surviving group watched in horror as their new neighbors began to transform into flesh-hungry monsters. They had no choice but to act fast if they wanted to avoid the same fate.

Gathering their belongings, the survivors made a run for it. They knew that they couldn't stay in the infected oasis, not even for a moment longer. They were left with no other option but to keep moving forward, seeking shelter as they went.

Their journey was long and tiring. Supplies were running low and danger lurked around every corner. But despite it all, the group persevered, motivated by their intense desire for survival.

They traversed through blistering hot deserts and treacherous mountain ranges, following maps and compasses towards a destination that none of them knew for sure even existed.

It was on one particularly dark night when everything changed.

As they settled into their makeshift camp, huddled together around a small fire, they heard a sound in the distance. A sound that chilled them to the bone.

It was the unmistakable sound of zombies.

Panicked and terrified, the survivors quickly gathered their belongings and began to run in the opposite direction. But soon enough, there were too many of them - too many zombies closing in on them from every angle.

In what felt like the final moments, when all hope seemed lost, a ray of light appeared in the darkness. A small army of survivors emerged from out of nowhere with weapons at the ready, fighting off the zombies with a fierce determination.

The two groups banded together, forming an alliance that quickly proved to be stronger than either of them could have imagined.

The survivors were caught off guard, and they quickly realized that the situation was hopeless. They knew they had to get out of the community before it was too late.

With heavy hearts, they gathered their supplies and made their way back out into the desert. They had no idea where they were going, or what they would find when they got there, but they knew that they couldn't stay in one place for too long.

As they walked, the sun beat down on them mercilessly, and their water supplies began to dwindle. They stumbled through the sand and rocks, their feet blistered and sore from days of walking.

But even as their bodies weakened, their spirits remained unbroken. They refused to give up hope - not after everything they'd been through.

Days turned into weeks, and still they walked. Every once in a while, they would come across a small town or village, but these places were just as dangerous as any other.

They learned to be cautious, approaching every new location with eyes wide open and guns at the ready.

It was a hard life, but it was all they had. And as long as they were together - fighting for survival against all odds - there was still hope for a better tomorrow.

The survivors continued their journey through the desert, never knowing what might be around the next bend. But they walked on, driven by a fierce determination to survive in a world that had been turned upside down by the Tranq virus.

And though the road ahead was long and uncertain - filled with danger and uncertainty at every turn - they knew that as long as they had each other, they could face anything that came their way.

The survivors were caught off guard, unable to comprehend what was happening. They had thought they were finally safe but now it seemed like they were back to square one.

The new strain of Tranq zombies was unlike any the survivors had encountered before. They were faster, stronger, and more vicious. They seemed to work together with a single-minded focus on killing the remaining humans.

The survivors fought back bravely, but it was a losing battle. One by one, their numbers dwindled as the zombies closed in, tearing them apart with terrifying speed and efficiency.

As the last of the survivors fell, one man stood alone in the middle of the chaos. He had managed to survive for this long by staying alert and keeping his wits about him.

But now, as he watched the zombies closing in around him, he knew that his time had come.

With a sense of grim resignation, he raised his weapon and prepared to make his final stand. But just as he was about to be overrun by the horde, something miraculous happened.

The zombies suddenly stopped in their tracks, frozen in place as if under some unseen spell. The man couldn't believe what he was seeing - it was like they had all been turned to stone.

And then he saw her - a figure standing at the edge of the oasis, her hands outstretched as if controlling the zombies with some sort of supernatural power.

She was beautiful in an otherworldly way, with thick raven hair and dark eyes that seemed to look right through him. As their eyes met, she gave him a small smile before turning and disappearing into the wasteland beyond.

The man knew that he had no way out.

Los Angeles

Tranq zombies invade Los Angeles.The city was in chaos, with hordes of undead roaming the streets, tearing apart anything in their path. The survivors who had managed to avoid the initial wave of infection were holed up in barricaded buildings, trying their best to stay alive.

But with supplies running low and the zombies multiplying by the minute, it was only a matter of time before their sanctuary was breached.

One group of survivors had taken refuge in an old movie theater on the outskirts of the city. They had managed to seal off the entrances and fortify the building as best as they could, but their situation was dire.

As they waited for the inevitable, tensions ran high. The survivors bickered and argued, unable to agree on what their next move should be.

But then she appeared - the woman from the oasis. She walked calmly into the theater, as if she had been expecting them.

At first, the survivors were skeptical. They didn't know who this woman was or where she had come from. But there was something about her that seemed different - something that gave them hope.

She sat down with them and told them her story. She had been born with a rare gift - the ability to control the dead. At first, she had tried to use this gift for good, to help those who were suffering. But when the Tranq virus hit, everything changed.

Now, she knew that she was their only hope. With her power, she could control the zombies and lead them away from the survivors' location.

The group listened intently as she explained her plan. It was risky - there was no guarantee that her power would work on such a large scale.

The city was plunged into chaos as the zombie horde made its way through the streets, tearing apart everything in its path.

People ran in all directions, their screams drowned out by the sound of gunfire and the guttural growls of the undead.

As the survivors took cover in buildings and alleyways, they knew that they were up against an enemy that could not be reasoned with - an enemy that would stop at nothing to consume them.

But even in the midst of all this horror and destruction, there were pockets of resistance. People who refused to give up without a fight.

One such group had taken refuge in an abandoned warehouse on the outskirts of the city. They had managed to gather enough supplies to last for a while, but they knew that they couldn't stay hidden forever.

Despite their fear and uncertainty, they banded together, determined to find a way to fight back against the zombie invasion.

Their leader was a woman named Ella - a tough-as-nails survivor who had been through hell and back more times than she cared to remember. She was a natural leader, respected by her comrades and feared by her enemies.

Under her guidance, the group began to fortify their position, barricading windows and doors and setting up traps to slow down any zombies that came their way.

They trained tirelessly, honing their skills with whatever weapons they could find - knives, guns, even makeshift bombs. They knew that they were vastly outnumbered, but they refused to let that stop them from trying to push back against the zombie horde.

Days turned into weeks, and still they fought on. The group's ranks swelled as more survivors made their way there.

The city that was once a bustling metropolis was now a post-apocalyptic wasteland. The streets were almost empty, except for the occasional pack of zombies roaming around.

But there were still survivors, huddled together in makeshift shelters, doing whatever they could to stay alive in the face of the terrifying threat.

One such group was led by a woman named Rachel - a fierce and determined leader who had managed to keep her people alive despite overwhelming odds.

Rachel knew that they couldn't stay where they were forever. They needed to find a way to get out of the city before it was too late.

So she gathered her most trusted advisors and began to devise a plan. They would have to move carefully and cautiously, avoiding the zombies wherever possible and fighting them off when necessary.

It wouldn't be easy, but Rachel was convinced that with enough determination and hard work, they would be able to make it out alive.

And so they set off into the heart of the infected city, weapons at the ready and nerves of steel. They moved through abandoned buildings and shattered neighborhoods, always keeping their eyes peeled for any sign of danger.

At first, it seemed like they might actually make it. They managed to avoid most of the zombies, fighting off those that got too close with deadly efficiency.

But then they encountered something unexpected - a group of humans who had turned on each other in their desperation to survive.

These people were just as dangerous as any zombie they'd faced before, attacking without mercy or remorse. Rachel's group fought back fiercely, but it quickly became clear that they were outnumbered and outmatched.

In the end, only a handful of them survived.

The city that once thrived with life and opportunity was now desolate and abandoned, with the undead roaming the streets in search of their next meal.

The few remaining survivors huddled together in small groups, barricading themselves inside buildings and scavenging for food and supplies whenever they could.

But even with their weapons and their wits, they knew that it was only a matter of time before they too succumbed to the virus.

It seemed that all hope was lost until a group of scientists stumbled upon a possible cure for the Tranq virus. They had been holed up in a secret laboratory, working tirelessly to find a way to reverse the effects of the deadly disease.

With their discovery, they created an antidote that brought the infected back to human form. It was then up to the survivors to distribute this cure throughout the city and save as many lives as possible.

And so, armed with vials of the antidote, they set out into the fray - risking their lives to save those who had fallen victim to the virus.

It was a dangerous mission, but one that gave them purpose amidst all the chaos. They fought their way through hordes of zombies, jumping over debris and dodging attacks from every direction.

But eventually, they succeeded. One by one, the infected were restored to normalcy. The city slowly began to come back to life - though there was still much work to be done.

As for the mysterious woman who had controlled the zombies with her supernatural abilities? She had disappeared into thin air, leaving behind only unanswered questions and a trail of confusion.

But even without her help, the survivors knew that they could overcome any obstacle.

Los Angeles soon became a shell of its former self. The once-thriving city was now just a shadow of its former glory. But amidst the despair and ruin, a new beacon of hope emerged.

A young woman named Jade had come to the city with a singular focus: to bring order to the chaos and establish a new government to lead the survivors.

She had an unshakable determination and charisma that quickly garnered her a following among the people. They saw her as a symbol of what they could be - strong, resilient, and capable of rising from the ashes of destruction.

With Jade's guidance, they started rebuilding damaged buildings, establishing supply lines, and creating safe zones for those who were still in hiding. It was no easy feat, but their determination never wavered.

As time passed, Jade's campaign against the zombie hordes began to pay off. Their numbers slowly dwindled as the cure reached more and more infected individuals.

It wasn't long before they were able to reclaim lost territory and begin expanding once again. The city was slowly but surely returning to its former glory.

Jade became known as the "Queen of Los Angeles," leading her people with an iron fist but also with compassion and empathy. She gave them hope where there was once only despair.

The apocalypse had taken so much from them - loved ones, homes, security - but it had also given them something they didn't have before: each other. They had come together in times of need and found strength in one another.

And as time marched on, the survivors knew that no matter what came their way, they would face it together, united under Jade's leadership.

The skyscrapers that once proudly scraped the sky were now nothing more than hollow reminders of a lost civilization. It was a city in ruins, where once there had been glitz and glamour, now there were only the ruins of what it had been.

The people who once called it home were now scattered across the world seeking refuge from the global catastrophe that had befallen them.

But, despite all the destruction and devastation, there were still those who remained in Los Angeles - those who refused to abandon the city they loved.

One such group was led by a man who had lost everything in the outbreak. His name was Max, and he was a former Marine turned leader of a ragtag team of survivors.

Max was a man of few words - tough, stoic, and determined. He had seen things that would make most people crumble, yet he remained unflappable.

Under his guidance, the survivors banded together in one of the few remaining buildings still standing. They fortified their position and braced themselves for whatever came next.

It wasn't easy - resources were scarce and danger lurked around every corner. But Max refused to give up. He was determined to keep his people safe no matter what it took.

And so they fought on, day after day, night after night. They scavenged for food and supplies wherever they could find them, always on the lookout for any signs of danger.

But as time went on, something began to change. The zombies that once flooded the streets began to get fewer and farther between.

It was as if something had driven them away - some force they could not see or comprehend.

The city's famous palm trees were now withered and dead, the once glorious Hollywood sign lay in ruins, and the streets were barren except for a few stranded cars.

The only sound that could be heard was the gentle humming of generators as the remaining survivors tried to keep some sense of normalcy.

They had managed to rebuild a small community, working together to fend off roaming zombie hordes and scavenging for whatever supplies they could find.

But despite their best efforts, the threat of the virus still loomed over them.

One day, they received a message - someone claiming to have information on how to permanently eradicate the virus had reached out to them.

It seemed too good to be true, but the survivors knew that they had nothing left to lose. They risked everything to make contact with this mysterious figure, hoping that this could finally be the answer they've been searching for.

The meeting place was set for the old Griffith Observatory - a risky move given its location in the center of an infected area. But they couldn't turn down any opportunity that might bring a glimmer of hope back into their lives.

As they cautiously made their way through the deserted streets, they noticed something odd. There were no zombies around - not even a single growl or moan could be heard.

But instead of feeling relieved, their instincts told them to tread more carefully. This silence was unsettling and it could only mean one thing: a trap was waiting for them.

Their intuition was right. As soon as they arrived at the observatory, they were ambushed by a group of heavily armed men. The survivalists didn't stand a chance against their superior firepower.

The streets were littered with debris, and the once beautiful buildings that had lined the city's skyline were now just crumbling ruins. The survivors moved through this wasteland, determined to rebuild their lives.

For Ella and Rachel's groups, the focus was on building a new community from the ground up. They worked together to clear out the rubble and set up new homes, using whatever resources they could find.

It was slow going at first, but eventually they managed to establish a semblance of normalcy. They set up small shops and businesses, working hard to create a sense of community and rebuild their shattered lives.

The scientists who had discovered the cure for the Tranq virus also played an important role in this rebuilding effort. With the threat of the virus finally eradicated, they worked tirelessly to develop better vaccines and tools to prevent future outbreaks.

The city slowly began to come back to life. People moved back into their homes, businesses reopened, and there was a newfound sense of hope in the air.

For years after the outbreak, Los Angeles remained a symbol of survival in the face of adversity. The people who had lived through that terrifying time banded together to create a new world - one that was stronger, more resilient, and filled with hope for the future.

NYC

Tranq zombies invade New York City. The streets of New York City were once filled with the hustle and bustle of daily life. But now, they were eerily quiet - the only sounds echoing through the abandoned buildings were the shuffling footsteps of the Tranq zombies.

For weeks now, the virus had been running rampant throughout the city, infecting anyone it came into contact with. The government had tried to contain it, but they were no match for the relentless horde that seemed to be spreading like wildfire.

The survivors knew that they needed to band together if they were going to have any chance of survival. They formed small groups, scavenging for supplies and weapons wherever they could find them.

But even with their combined strength, it seemed like a losing battle. The zombies were everywhere, lurking around every corner and waiting to pounce on unsuspecting victims.

One group, led by a woman named Ava, took a different approach. Instead of fighting back against the zombies, they tried to blend in with them.

They covered themselves in dirt and grime, mimicking the zombie's shuffling gait and avoiding eye contact at all costs. It was a dangerous strategy - if they were caught, they would be torn apart in an instant.

But surprisingly, it seemed to be working. The zombies didn't seem to recognize them as human and would often let them pass by without incident.

It wasn't an ideal solution - they still had to scavenge for food and supplies during moments of vulnerability - but it was better than facing constant attacks from the zombie horde.

As time passed, Ava's group made some unlikely allies. A small team of army soldiers had managed to avoid infection.

The once bustling city streets were now eerily quiet, the sound of shuffling feet and low growling replacing the sounds of honking cars and people rushing past each other.

As the outbreak of the Tranq virus hit New York City, people quickly began to fall ill and turn into zombies. Panic spread like wildfire as the city was plunged into chaos.

But amidst all the destruction, there were some who refused to give up hope. One such person was Sarah, a nurse who had worked in one of the city's hospitals before the outbreak.

With her medical training and her unshakable determination, Sarah quickly became a leader among the survivors. She gathered people together and established a safe zone in one of the remaining buildings.

It was not an easy task, but Sarah worked tirelessly day and night to ensure the safety of her group. They scavenged for food and supplies wherever they could find them, constantly on guard against any signs of danger.

But despite their best efforts, they could see that they were outnumbered. The zombies seemed to be everywhere, swarming through the streets like a sea of undead flesh.

It was then that Sarah realized that they needed help - outside help. She contacted anyone she could think of - military personnel, scientists, anyone - in hopes that someone would be able to provide them with the tools they needed to fight back against this zombie army.

Days turned into weeks, and weeks turned into months. The survivors continued to fight on, even as their numbers dwindled and their resources ran low. But still, hope remained alive within them.

And then one day, Sarah received a response to her call for help.

The Big Apple was no match for the Tranq virus. Within days, the streets filled with the walking dead, their hunger insatiable and their numbers growing with each passing moment.

But there were pockets of survivors who refused to give up without a fight. They band together in desperate attempts to protect themselves from the zombies that lurked around every corner.

Among them was a young woman named Maya. She had lost everything - her family, her home, and all sense of security. But she refused to let the zombies win.

Maya quickly became a leader among the survivors. Her unrelenting determination and quick-thinking saved countless lives, and soon she had a following of people who looked up to her with reverence.

Together, they worked tirelessly to find ways to fend off the hordes of zombies that threatened their very existence. They scavenged for food and supplies wherever they could find them, always keeping one step ahead of the relentless undead.

And as time went on, they became more organized and methodical in their efforts. They set up traps to lure zombies away from populated areas and fortified their positions whenever possible.

But even with all their efforts, it seemed that there was no end in sight. The zombies kept coming, their numbers growing by the day.

It wasn't until they received an unexpected message that things began to change. A group of scientists claimed to have discovered a cure for the Tranq virus - something that could finally put an end to the zombie apocalypse once and for all.

Maya didn't hesitate for a moment. She led her people on a dangerous journey across the city to find these scientists, fighting off zombie hordes along the way.

New York City had been hit hard by the Tranq virus. It had started with a few isolated cases, but before long the city was overrun with the undead.

The streets were empty except for the shambling hordes of zombies that roamed the city, searching for their next meal.

In the midst of this chaos was a group of survivors led by a young woman named Ava. She was a former nurse who had seen firsthand the devastation that the virus had wrought.

Ava knew that if they were going to survive, they would need to band together and work as a team. They set up a base in an abandoned building and began fortifying it against the incoming zombie hordes.

It wasn't long before they realized that they were not alone. Other small groups of survivors had managed to make it this far and were now looking for shelter and safety.

Ava welcomed them all, knowing that their chances of survival were better if they stood together.

As days turned into weeks, the survivors worked tirelessly to clear out the infected areas and reclaim parts of the city. They scoured abandoned stores and buildings for supplies, always on high alert for any signs of danger.

But despite their best efforts, they couldn't contain the virus. It continued to spread unchecked, taking down more and more people each day.

Ava knew that something had to be done. She rallied her fellow survivors, determined to come up with a plan to rid the city of the zombie threat once and for all.

They scoured through old newspapers, government documents, and other sources to try and find any information on how to fight back against this new enemy.

Their search led them to a skyscraper in Manhattan.

The building was unlike any other Ava and her group had seen before. It was tall, with mirrored windows that made it impossible to see inside.

Ava knew that they needed to investigate this building - it could hold the key to saving their city.

They crept through the deserted streets, avoiding the zombie hordes as they made their way to the base of the skyscraper. As they approached, they noticed that the doors were unlocked - a clear invitation.

Inside, they found a high-tech laboratory filled with scientists and researchers. These were not ordinary scientists - they were working on a secret government project that had been kept hidden from the public eye.

They explained to Ava and her group that they had been working on a vaccine for the Tranq virus, and that it was almost complete.

Ava couldn't believe it - after all this time, there was finally hope.

The scientists handed over the vaccine, along with a team of soldiers who would help protect them as they made their way back to their base.

It wasn't easy - the zombie hordes were relentless, and Ava's group had to fight their way through the streets. But finally, they made it back to their base.

The vaccine worked. One by one, the survivors were vaccinated against the virus, and slowly but surely, the city began to come back to life.

Ava knew that there was still much work to be done - rebuilding their city, searching for more survivors, and making sure that something like this never happened again.

But for now, she allowed herself a small moment of relief. The worst was over, and hope had been restored.

The group of survivors, led by Ava, cautiously made their way through the deserted streets towards the skyscraper. As they approached the building, they could see that it was heavily guarded by soldiers in full combat gear.

Ava stepped forward and called out to the soldiers, explaining their situation and pleading with them to let them inside. The soldiers looked at them skeptically but eventually agreed to let them in.

Inside the building, Ava was introduced to the leader of the military operation - a stern-looking man named Colonel Jackson. He listened carefully as Ava explained their plan to eradicate the zombie virus from New York City.

Colonel Jackson was impressed with Ava's bravery and determination. He agreed to provide her with a team of soldiers and any resources she needed to carry out her mission.

Together, Ava and her team worked tirelessly to clear out infected areas and destroy any zombie hordes in their way. They developed new weapons and strategies, constantly adapting to stay ahead of the undead threat.

Days turned into weeks, and finally, they had cleared out all of Manhattan. The survivors could finally breathe a sigh of relief knowing that they had beaten back the zombie horde.

But Ava knew that there was still work to be done. They had to find a way to prevent another outbreak from happening again. She worked closely with Colonel Jackson and the scientists who had developed a cure for the virus to create a plan for long-term prevention.

Finally, after months of hard work, they were able not only to cure those infected with the virus but also prevent any future outbreaks from occurring.

New York City slowly began to recover from the devastation of the zombie apocalypse.

And then they woke up and realized that they were dreaming and the city was in fact overrun by Tranq zombies.

It was there that they met a man named Dr. Robert Thompson. He was a former CDC scientist who had been working on a cure for the Tranq virus before the outbreak.

Dr. Thompson had been holed up in the skyscraper for months, working tirelessly to finish his research. When Ava and her group arrived, he was hesitant to let them in.

But Ava was determined. She convinced Dr. Thompson that they were all on the same side - that they all wanted to find a way to end this zombie apocalypse once and for all.

Slowly but surely, Dr. Thompson began to open up to them. He showed them his research, which was more advanced than anything they had ever seen before.

With his help, the survivors began to formulate a plan. They would gather all the supplies they needed and create a safe zone around Dr. Thompson's lab.

They worked day and night, fighting off zombie hordes and gathering as many supplies as they could find.

But even with their efforts, it seemed like an impossible task. The zombies were everywhere, always one step ahead of them.

It wasn't until Dr. Thompson completed his research that things began to change. He had found a cure for the Tranq virus - something that could finally put an end to the zombie apocalypse once and for all.

The survivors rejoiced at the news, knowing that this was the breakthrough they had been waiting for. They gathered together in Dr. Thompson's lab, watching as he prepared the first doses of the cure.

As each person received their shot, they felt a sense of relief wash over them. They knew that their days of living in fear and uncertainty.

Ava and her group knew that this was a dangerous but necessary task. They had to make their way up to the top of the skyscraper to find the answers they needed.

The journey was treacherous, with zombie hordes lurking around every corner. The survivors fought their way through wave after wave of the undead, never losing hope that they would make it to the top.

When they finally reached the upper floors of the skyscraper, they found a group of scientists who had been holed up there for months, working on a cure for the virus.

Ava and her group quickly joined forces with the scientists, pooling their resources and knowledge to come up with a plan. They worked tirelessly day and night, determined to find a way to save the city from the zombie apocalypse.

Finally, after weeks of research and experimentation, they discovered a cure. It was risky, and there was no guarantee that it would work, but they knew they had to try.

Ava and her fellow survivors ventured out into the city once again, this time armed with vials of the cure. They fought their way through wave after wave of zombies, never losing sight of their goal.

As they made their way through the city, administering the cure to as many people as they could find, something miraculous happened - the infected began to regain their humanity.

Slowly but surely, the streets began to fill with people once again. The zombie hordes dwindled until they were nothing but a memory.

In the end, Ava and her group had succeeded in saving New York City from certain doom. They had shown that even in the darkest hour, hope could still prevail.

No, there is no hope.

Philly

Philadelphia is invaded by Tranq zombies. Ava and her group had already been through one zombie apocalypse, but they had never seen anything like the Tranq zombies. These zombies moved with a strange, slow grace - almost as if they were underwater.

At first, the survivors tried to fight back like they had before, using weapons and brute force. But it quickly became clear that this wasn't going to work against the Tranq zombies.

The survivors began to realize that they needed a new strategy. They started researching the Tranq virus, trying to figure out how it worked and how they could stop it.

As they worked, Ava couldn't help but feel a sense of despair. It seemed like there was no hope of stopping these zombies - they were unlike anything she had ever seen before.

But then one day, Ava stumbled upon a strange discovery. She found an old research paper that suggested there might be a weakness in the Tranq virus - something that could be exploited to stop the zombies.

Ava and her group poured over this paper, trying to figure out what the weakness was and how they could use it against the Tranq zombies.

Finally, after weeks of work, they came up with a plan. They would create a specialized bomb that could target the weakness in the virus and destroy it once and for all.

It was an incredibly risky plan - there was no guarantee that it would work. But Ava knew that it was their only hope.

The group worked tirelessly to create the bomb, using every bit of knowledge they had about the virus and its weaknesses. Finally, after what felt like an eternity, they had a working prototype.

Ava and her team ventured out into the city once again.

The once-bustling streets of Philadelphia were now eerily quiet, save for the occasional sound of groaning from the hordes of Tranq zombies that roamed the city. The survivors who remained huddled together in small groups, desperately searching for a way out.

Among them was a young woman named Sarah, who had lost almost everything in the outbreak. Her family and friends were either dead or turned into mindless zombies. But Sarah refused to give up hope. She knew that somewhere out there, there had to be a way to stop the virus from spreading.

One day, while scavenging for supplies, Sarah stumbled upon an old laboratory in the heart of the city. Inside, she found a team of scientists who had been working on a cure for the Tranq virus.

At first, the scientists were hesitant to let Sarah in. They had been working in secret for fear of being overrun by the zombies outside. But Sarah was determined to help in any way she could.

Together, they worked tirelessly day and night, testing new formulas and treatments until they finally found a cure.

It wasn't easy getting the word out to other survivors - they had to navigate through dangerous and infested areas to reach as many people as possible. But eventually, they managed to administer the cure to those in need.

The city slowly began to come back to life. The sound of reviving city echoed through deserted streets. The zombie hordes dwindled until they too were cured.

Sarah became something of a hero among the survivors, a symbol of hope and perseverance in even the darkest times. And though she knew that there was still much work to be done.

The streets of Philadelphia were once bustling with life, but now they were empty, save for the endless hordes of Tranq zombies that roamed aimlessly. The city had been overrun and nearly all hope seemed lost.

But there were a few survivors left. Among them was a woman named Maria, who had managed to barricade herself inside an abandoned warehouse. She had been surviving on scraps of food and water for weeks, constantly on the lookout for any signs of life outside.

One day, as she was scavenging for supplies in the nearby area, she stumbled upon a group of survivors huddled together in a nearby alleyway. They were all terrified, having narrowly escaped from a massive horde of Tranq zombies.

Maria knew that she couldn't leave them to fend for themselves. She cautiously approached them and explained her situation, offering to take them back to her warehouse where they could regroup and come up with a plan.

The survivors reluctantly agreed and followed Maria back to the warehouse. Together, they worked to fortify their space, setting up traps and making sure that no zombies could make their way inside.

Days turned into weeks as they waited out the zombie apocalypse. Maria and her group had enough supplies to last them for a while, but they knew that eventually they would have to venture out into the dangerous city in search of more food and water.

They mapped out a plan, deciding which areas of the city were safe to travel through and which areas were too overrun by zombies.

But their plans were quickly thwarted when they stumbled upon a massive horde of Tranq zombies while out on a supply run. They ran as fast as they could, but the zombies were too fast.

The streets of Philadelphia were deserted, save for the countless Tranq zombies that roamed aimlessly through the city. The survivors were few and far between, and the odds of finding anyone alive seemed slim.

But Ava and her group were determined to survive. They had learned from their experience in New York City and knew that they needed to stick together if they were going to make it through the apocalypse.

They scavenged for food and supplies, avoiding the zombies as much as possible. But it seemed like they were always one step behind - every time they found a safe place to hide, the zombies would find them again.

It wasn't until they stumbled upon an abandoned military base that things began to look up. The base was loaded with weapons and supplies, enough to keep them alive for months if they played their cards right.

Ava took charge, organizing the group and formulating a plan. They would use what resources they had to fortify the base, creating a safe zone that would keep the zombies out.

It wasn't easy - they had to fight off wave after wave of zombies, losing some members of their group along the way. But finally, they succeeded in creating a secure perimeter around the base, free from any undead threat.

For weeks, they lived within the walls of the base, never venturing outside except to scavenge for supplies. It was a bleak existence, but it kept them alive.

And then one day, something miraculous happened. One of their own was bitten by a Tranq zombie, but instead of turning into one herself, she began to show signs of recovery.

Ava and her group couldn't believe their eyes as they watched their infected comrade's condition improve. It seemed like a miracle, but they soon realized that there was more to it than that.

After conducting some experiments, they discovered that the virus was mutating within their friend's body, adapting itself to become less lethal.

Ava and her team saw this as an opportunity - if they could replicate this mutation in others, then maybe they could find a way to end the apocalypse for good.

They began experimenting on themselves, injecting themselves with small doses of the Tranq virus in the hopes of triggering a similar mutation. It wasn't easy - many of them became severely ill and some even died.

But finally, after months of trial and error, Ava and her team found a way to trigger the desired mutation. They had done it. They had found a cure for the Tranq virus.

With renewed hope, Ava and her team set out to spread the cure throughout the city. They ventured far and wide, administering the cure to anyone they came across who had been infected with the virus.

Eventually, their efforts paid off - the streets of Philadelphia were no longer empty. The survivors began to band together once again, rebuilding their homes and communities.

It would take years for the city to fully recover from the apocalypse, but Ava and her team had done something incredible - they had saved countless lives and given hope back to a world that had lost it.

At first, Ava and the others were skeptical - they had never seen anything like it before. But as the days passed, the woman continued to improve. Her fever subsided, and the wound from the bite slowly began to heal.

Excited by this discovery, Ava and her team began to experiment. They injected small amounts of the Tranq virus into other members of their group, hoping to replicate the strange phenomenon.

To their amazement, it worked. Each person that was infected with the virus showed signs of recovery, slowly returning to their normal selves instead of turning into a zombie.

Ava knew that this could be the key to stopping the apocalypse once and for all. She worked tirelessly with her team, developing a cure using small amounts of the Tranq virus as a base.

It wasn't easy - they had to test and re-test the formula over and over again, making sure that it was safe and effective. But finally, they succeeded. They had created a cure for the Tranq virus.

And with that cure in hand, Ava and her team ventured out into the city once more. They sought out other survivors, administering the cure to those who had been infected by the virus.

For weeks they worked, traveling from one end of Philadelphia to the other in search of those in need. And slowly but surely, they began to see a change.

The streets once again became alive with the sound of humanity. The zombie hordes dwindled and eventually disappeared as more and more people were cured of the virus.

In time, life returned to Philadelphia. The survivors came together, forming new communities and rebuilding what had been lost.

Ava and her group were shocked - they had never seen anything like it before. The woman, named Lena, had been bitten by a Tranq zombie two days prior, and they had all assumed that she was going to turn just like their friends and family members who had been bitten before her.

But instead of succumbing to the virus, Lena's body seemed to be fighting it off. Her wounds were healing at an incredible rate, and she was showing no signs of turning.

Ava and her group were overjoyed at the discovery. They knew that if they could figure out what was different about Lena's immune system, they might be able to find a cure for the Tranq virus.

They set up a makeshift laboratory within the walls of the military base, using their limited knowledge of medical science to study Lena's blood and tissues.

Days turned into weeks as they worked tirelessly on their research, barely stopping to eat or sleep. But finally, after what felt like an eternity, they had a breakthrough.

They discovered that Lena's immune system had somehow developed a resistance to the virus - something that they had never seen before in anyone else who had been bitten.

Using this information, Ava and her group worked around the clock to create a vaccine that could replicate Lena's resistance within other survivors' bodies.

It wasn't easy - the resources available to them were limited, and they only had one chance to get it right. But finally, after weeks of work, they had a working vaccine.

They tested it on themselves first, injecting the serum into their own bodies with shaking hands. And then they waited.

Hours ticked by as they waited for any sign of it working.

Ava and her group were stunned. They had never seen anything like it before. At first, they thought it was a fluke, but as days passed, the woman continued to heal.

It was a glimmer of hope for the survivors - a possible way to reverse the effects of the Tranq virus. The group studied the woman's blood and discovered a unique antibody that seemed to fight against the virus.

They worked around the clock to produce more of this antibody, hoping to create a cure for the virus. It was a long shot, but they had nothing else to lose.

After weeks of work, they had a viable cure. Ava and her team ventured out into the city once again, administering the cure to those in need.

Slowly but surely, they began to see signs of life returning to Philadelphia. People emerged from hiding places, hopeful for a future where they didn't have to fear the undead.

Ava and her team became heroes among the survivors - saviors who gave them a second chance at life. And though there were still zombies out there, the newfound hope among the survivors was something that couldn't be stopped.

Texas

Texas is invaded by Tranq zombies. The Tranq virus had finally made its way to Texas. It was impossible to know how it got there, but the devastation it had caused was already evident.

The once-vibrant cities were now ghost towns, with only the undead roaming the streets. The survivors who had managed to make it out alive were scattered and struggling to survive.

But amidst the chaos and destruction, there was a glimmer of hope. A small group of survivors had banded together in the heart of Texas, determined to find a way to defeat the Tranq zombies and reclaim their state from the undead.

They called themselves the Lone Star Resistance, and their leader was a fierce woman named Jessa. She had been a soldier before the apocalypse, and her training had come in handy during the early days of the outbreak.

Jessa and her team worked tirelessly to gather resources and recruit new members. They scoured every corner of Texas for survivors, offering them protection and a chance to fight back against the zombies.

It wasn't easy - the Tranq zombies were relentless, and supplies were scarce. But Jessa refused to give up. She knew that if they could find a way to stop the virus from spreading, then maybe they could turn the tide of the war.

And then it happened - they discovered a survivor who was immune to the virus. Just like Lena in Philadelphia, this woman's body was fighting off the Tranq virus, giving Jessa and her team hope that they might be able to create a cure.

They brought the woman back to their base and immediately began studying her blood and tissues. It was a challenge - they didn't have access to high-tech medical equipment.

The state of Texas had always been known for its fierce independence, but it was that same independence that proved to be its downfall when the Tranq virus hit.

One by one, cities and towns fell to the zombie hordes. The few survivors were forced to band together, fighting for their lives in a world gone mad.

But there was one group that refused to back down - a group of survivors led by a woman named Sarah.

She and her team had seen what the Tranq virus could do, but they were determined to fight back with everything they had. They scoured the state, searching for others who shared their determination to survive.

They found them in small pockets across Texas - men and women who were willing to risk their lives for the chance at a better tomorrow.

Together, the group fought back against the zombie hordes, using everything from guns to makeshift weapons to protect themselves.

It was a hard life - one where every day was a struggle to survive. But Sarah and her team refused to give up hope.

And then one day, everything changed.

As they were scavenging for supplies in an abandoned military base, they stumbled upon something that would change their fate forever - a stash of experimental vaccines created before the outbreak of the Tranq virus.

With trembling hands, Sarah and her team injected themselves with the vaccines, hoping beyond hope that it would be enough to save them.

Days turned into weeks as they waited for any sign of it working. But slowly but surely, they felt the effects - their wounds began to heal faster, and they became stronger and faster than ever before.

Encouraged by this development, Sarah and her team continued.

The sun was scorching hot as Ava and her team rode into Texas on their horses. The state had been hit hard by the Tranq virus, and hardly any survivors remained.

As they rode through the deserted streets, they saw nothing but abandoned cars and buildings torn apart by the undead.

But Ava wasn't deterred. She had done this before, administering her cure to survivors in Philadelphia. And she was determined to do it again.

They searched high and low for survivors, but each day seemed more hopeless than the last. They encountered few people, but those who remained were too far gone to be saved.

It wasn't until they stumbled upon a group of women and children holed up in an abandoned school that they finally found success. These were the first survivors that they had come across who seemed to be unaffected by the virus.

Ava was amazed - she had never seen anything like it before. These people were living proof that there was a way to survive without succumbing to the virus.

She examined their blood and discovered that they carried a unique enzyme that seemed to fight against the virus. Using this information, Ava worked with her team to create a vaccine using the enzyme as its base.

It took weeks of hard work, but they eventually had a cure that could potentially save countless lives. They set out into Texas once again, distributing the vaccine to anyone they came across who had been affected by the virus.

Slowly but surely, life returned to Texas. Survivors emerged from their hiding places, thankful for a second chance at life. And though there were still dangers out there - both from the zombies and from other survivors - Ava and her group.

The Tranq virus had spread like wildfire throughout Texas, leaving nothing but death and destruction in its wake. The streets once filled with bustling cities and towns were now overrun by hordes of zombies, their eyes glazed over and minds consumed by the virus.

Ava had been on the road when she first heard about the outbreak. She had been traveling through the southern parts of the United States, searching for survivors and trying to make a difference in any way that she could.

Within days, she found herself at the center of a massive zombie horde. The creatures had surrounded her car, their hands clawing at the windows as they tried to break through.

With no other choice, Ava abandoned her vehicle and ran for her life. She was forced to fight her way through wave after wave of zombies, her heart pounding in her chest as she frantically searched for a place to hide.

Days turned into weeks as Ava struggled to survive in the new world order. She scrounged for food and water wherever she could find it, always on the move and always on the lookout for any sign of other survivors.

But despite her best efforts, Ava found herself becoming more and more isolated as time passed. The world around her had become a desolate wasteland, with nothing but death and destruction at every turn.

It wasn't until she stumbled upon an abandoned military base that Ava finally found a glimmer of hope. The base was heavily fortified, with reinforced walls and enough supplies to last for months.

At first, Ava thought it was too good to be true - surely there had to be some kind of catch?

But as she explored the base further, she realized it was no alone.

A group of survivors, led by a man named Jack, had made the base their home. They welcomed Ava with open arms, eagerly offering her food and shelter.

Ava was grateful to have finally found a community of survivors. Together, they worked to fortify the base and defend themselves against the zombie hordes that threatened their safety.

It wasn't easy - the zombies seemed to be never-ending in number, and the walls of the base were constantly under attack. But Ava found strength in the resilience of her new friends.

Days turned into weeks, and then into months. Slowly but surely, the survivors at the base began to rebuild their world from the ashes of what had been destroyed.

They grew crops in the fields outside the walls, using rainwater collected in barrels for irrigation. They even managed to rig up a solar-powered generator, providing them with a source of electricity for lights and communication equipment.

As time passed, Ava found herself falling in love with Jack. He was strong and kindhearted, always putting the needs of others before his own. And despite everything they had been through, he still believed that there was hope for a better future.

One night, as they stood watch together on the walls of the base, Ava turned to him and whispered, "I don't want to just survive anymore. I want to live."

Jack smiled at her, placing a hand on her shoulder. "We will," he said. "I promise you."

And for the first time since the outbreak began, Ava felt a sense of hope stirring inside her heart. Together with Jack and their fellow survivors, she knew that they could build a new world.

There were other survivors like her, huddled together in makeshift living quarters, all of them looking up at Ava expectantly. They had heard that someone was coming, and they couldn't believe their luck when they saw her.

Ava felt a surge of hope well up inside her as she looked around at the people gathered there. For the first time in weeks, she wasn't alone anymore.

She quickly got to work, helping the survivors fortify their base and gather supplies. They worked tirelessly day after day, doing everything they could to ensure their survival in a world overrun by the undead.

And then one day, they received a distress call over the radio - a group of survivors was trapped in a nearby town, surrounded by zombies and running out of food and water.

Without hesitation, Ava and a small team set out to rescue them. It was a dangerous mission - the town was swarming with Tranq zombies. But Ava knew that they had to try.

They fought their way through the streets, gunfire ringing out as they took down zombie after zombie. It was touch and go for a while, but eventually Ava and her team managed to reach the survivors and bring them back to the military base.

It was a turning point for Ava and her group. They realized that there were still people alive out there who needed their help. And so they set out once again into the dangerous unknown, determined to find other survivors and help them in any way they could.

As they traveled through Texas, they encountered more and more people who were fighting for their lives against the zombie hordes. Some had barricaded themselves in abandoned buildings, while others were on the move.

There was a group of survivors living within the walls, led by a strong and determined woman named Jessa. They had banded together, pooling their resources and fighting back against the zombie hordes.

Ava felt a sense of relief wash over her - for the first time in weeks, she felt safe. She quickly joined forces with Jessa and her team, working alongside them to fight back against the Tranq virus.

It wasn't easy - the zombies were relentless, and supplies were scarce. But Ava refused to give up. She was determined to find a way to stop the virus from spreading, no matter the cost.

And then Jessa made an incredible discovery - there was a survivor within their group who was immune to the virus.

Ava couldn't believe it - this was the breakthrough they had been hoping for. With this person's blood and tissues, they could potentially create a cure for the virus once and for all.

She worked tirelessly alongside Jessa and her team, using their limited resources to study the immune survivor's blood and develop a vaccine that could potentially save countless lives.

It was a race against time - every day, more and more people were falling victim to the virus. But with Ava's expertise and Jessa's leadership, they managed to create a vaccine that could combat the Tranq virus.

They set out into Texas once again, distributing the vaccine to anyone they came across who had been affected by the virus.

Slowly but surely, life returned to Texas. Survivors emerged from their hiding places, thankful for a second chance at life. And though there were still dangers out there - both from the zombies and from other survivors.

There was a small community of survivors living within the base, led by a woman named Sophie. They had begun to build a life for themselves, forming alliances and working together in order to survive.

Sophie welcomed Ava into their community with open arms, and for the first time in weeks, Ava felt like she had found a place where she truly belonged.

Together, they worked to fortify the base even further, setting up traps and defenses to keep out the hordes of zombies that threatened to overrun them at any moment.

Despite the constant danger, Ava couldn't shake her determination to find a way to stop the virus from spreading. She spent hours poring over scientific documents and studying the medical equipment left behind at the base.

And then one day, she had a breakthrough. Buried in the back of an abandoned laboratory, Ava discovered an experimental vaccine that could potentially cure the Tranq virus once and for all.

With new hope lighting her way, Ava set out with Sophie and a small group of survivors on a dangerous mission through zombie-infested territory to find the ingredients necessary to create the vaccine.

It was a harrowing journey - they narrowly escaped death on multiple occasions as they fought off zombies and encountered hostile survivors who would stop at nothing to protect their own interests.

But finally, they succeeded. With shaking hands, Ava mixed together the ingredients for the vaccine and administered it to Sophie and her fellow survivors.

Days turned into weeks as they waited anxiously for any sign of its effectiveness. And then it happened - one by one, the survivors began to recover from their illnesses. Their wounds healed faster than before and their strength returned.

Ava and Sophie knew it wouldn't work because they had already tried and failed to create a cure in another state.

It doesn't make sense why people want to cure something that they already know has no cure. Some things just can't be cured.

Despite the setback, Ava refused to give up hope. She knew that there had to be a way to save humanity from the horrors of the Tranq virus.

She spent long hours deep in thought, pouring over scientific papers and schematics in search of a solution.

And then it hit her - if they couldn't find a cure for the virus, they could find a way to prevent it from ever happening in the first place.

With that realization, Ava set out to create a plan to prevent future outbreaks of the virus. She worked tirelessly alongside Sophie and other survivors, gathering resources and building alliances with other groups across Texas.

Slowly but surely, they began to implement their plan, setting up early warning systems and surveillance networks that could detect outbreaks before they became full-blown pandemics.

It was a long and difficult journey, but finally, they succeeded. The Tranq virus was eradicated from Texas, and soon after, from the rest of the country.

Ava looked out at the world from within the walls of the newly-rebuilt base, watching as people emerged from their hiding places and began to rebuild their lives.

It wasn't perfect - there were still dangers out there, both from zombies and other survivors. But for the first time in years, Ava felt like there was hope for a better future.

And with that hope filling her heart, she set out once again into the unknown, determined to make a difference in a world that had been broken by tragedy and despair.

But Ava couldn't give up. She had seen too much suffering and loss to simply accept that there was no hope. She continued her research, determined to find a way to save those who were still suffering.

One day, as she was studying the virus under a microscope, she noticed something strange. There was an anomaly in the virus's genetic code - something that shouldn't have been there.

Ava's heart raced as she realized what she had discovered. This wasn't just any virus - it had been genetically engineered.

With this newfound knowledge, Ava and her team worked tirelessly to find a way to create an antidote that could neutralize the virus's effects. And finally, after months of work, they succeeded.

The antidote wasn't a cure - it couldn't reverse the damage already done by the virus. But it could prevent the virus from spreading further and save countless lives in the process.

Ava and her team distributed the antidote throughout Texas, working tirelessly to ensure that everyone who needed it received it.

It wasn't easy - there were constant dangers and obstacles to overcome. But in time, life in Texas began to return to something resembling normalcy. People began to rebuild their homes and communities, and hope returned to the hearts of survivors.

And though there would always be dangers out there - both from zombies and from other survivors - Ava knew that as long as there were people willing to fight for a better world, there would always be hope.

But Ava and Sophie refused to give up. They knew that they had to keep trying, no matter how slim their chances of success might be.

And so they set out once again into the dangerous unknown, determined to find a way to stop the spread of the virus and protect those who were still alive.

As they traveled through the zombie-infested wasteland, Ava couldn't shake the feeling that they were being watched. She scanned their surroundings, her heart racing as she searched for any signs of danger.

And then she saw them - a group of survivors lurking in the shadows, watching their every move. Ava raised her weapon, ready to defend herself and her friends if necessary.

But as the survivors emerged from the shadows, Ava realized that they weren't hostile after all. In fact, they seemed almost...relieved to see her.

"We've been looking for you," one of them said. "We heard about your efforts to find a cure for the virus."

Ava was stunned. She had never expected anyone outside of her own group to know about their mission.

"We want to help," another survivor said. "We have skills that could be useful to you."

Feeling a sense of hope wash over her once again, Ava welcomed the newcomers into their group. With their combined skills and determination, perhaps they could finally find a way to stop the virus from spreading.

Days turned into weeks, and then into months. Ava and her fellow survivors worked tirelessly day and night, doing everything in their power to develop a cure for the Tranq virus.

It wasn't easy - there were setbacks and failures along the way. But they refused to give up hope.

Having hope for something that you know deep down is not possible is completely stupid.

But Ava couldn't give up hope. She knew that they had to keep trying, no matter how impossible it seemed.

And so she continued to work tirelessly, developing new ways to fight against the zombie hordes and researching new potential cures for the virus.

It was a long and difficult journey, but Ava refused to give up. She knew that as long as there was even the slightest chance of finding a cure, they had to keep fighting.

The future was uncertain, but one thing was clear - as long as Ava and her fellow survivors continued to work together, there was hope for a better tomorrow.

Arkansas

Tranq zombies invade Arkansas. The news of the outbreak in Arkansas spread quickly, and Ava knew that they had to act fast if they wanted to stop the virus from spreading further.

As she and her group made their way towards Arkansas, Ava couldn't shake the feeling of dread that settled in the pit of her stomach. They had fought for so long to eradicate the virus, but it seemed like every time they took a step forward, something pushed them two steps back.

But they refused to give up. They had come too far to let the virus win.

When they arrived in Arkansas, the situation was worse than they had feared. The Tranq virus had already spread further than anyone could have imagined, infecting entire communities and turning once-thriving cities into ghost towns.

Ava and her group worked tirelessly to clear out the infected areas and provide aid to any survivors they found along the way. It was an uphill battle, but with every zombie they took down and every survivor they helped, Ava felt a renewed sense of hope.

And then one day, as they were scavenging through an abandoned lab, Ava stumbled upon something that would change everything.

It was a notebook filled with cryptic notes and diagrams - details about a new strain of the Tranq virus that was even more deadly than the original. But there were also clues within the notes about how to create a vaccine that could neutralize the virus's effects.

Ava's heart raced as she realized what she was looking at. This could be it - the key to finally eradicating the virus once and for all.

With new determination fueling her every step, Ava and her team set out to find the necessary.

Ava and her team had received word of the outbreak in Arkansas and knew that they had to act fast. They packed their supplies and weapons and set out on the long journey to the neighboring state.

When they arrived, they were met with chaos. The streets were overrun with zombies, and panicked survivors were running in every direction.

Ava's heart raced as she realized the extent of the outbreak. It was worse than anything they had ever seen before.

But despite the danger, Ava and her team knew that they couldn't turn back now. They had a duty to help those in need and find a way to stop the spread of the virus once and for all.

They set up a base camp on the outskirts of town and immediately began scouting for survivors. It wasn't long before they came across a group of people who had barricaded themselves inside a local diner.

Ava approached them cautiously, her weapon at the ready. But to her surprise, they welcomed her and her team with open arms.

"We're glad you're here," one of them said. "We've been fighting off these damn zombies for days."

Ava listened intently as they told her about how the virus had spread through their town, turning their friends and family into mindless monsters.

She knew that time was running out. If they didn't act fast, the virus would continue to spread until there was no one left alive.

With grim determination, Ava and her team set out into the zombie-infested town, searching for any clues that could lead them to a cure.

Days turned into weeks, but still there was no sign of a cure. The zombies continued to multiply.

The news spread quickly throughout the state. People began to panic, barricading themselves inside their homes in a desperate bid to escape the virus.

Ava and her team heard the news and immediately set out for Arkansas. They knew that time was running out - if they didn't act fast, the virus could spread throughout the entire state.

As they made their way through the zombie-infested streets of Arkansas, Ava couldn't help but feel a sense of deja vu. It was as if they were back in Texas all over again, fighting against an enemy that seemed impossible to defeat.

But Ava refused to give up hope. She knew that they had to find a way to stop the virus from spreading, no matter what it took.

They worked tirelessly day and night, gathering resources and building alliances with other survivors across Arkansas. Slowly but surely, they began to implement their plan to stop the virus from spreading any further.

It wasn't easy - there were countless obstacles and dangers to overcome. But Ava and her team refused to give up hope.

Months turned into years, and slowly but surely, the virus began to recede. People emerged from their hiding places and began to rebuild their lives, grateful for the chance to start anew.

Ava smiled as she looked out at the world, watching as people continued to work together towards a brighter future.

It wasn't perfect - there were still dangers out there, both from zombies and from other survivors. But for the first time in years, Ava felt like there was hope for a better tomorrow.

Ava and her group had been on the move for weeks, searching for any signs of other survivors in the zombie-infested state of Arkansas.

Their supplies were dwindling, and morale was low. It seemed like their mission to find a cure for the Tranq virus was becoming more impossible by the day.

But Ava refused to give up. She knew that they had to keep pushing forward, no matter how difficult it became.

As they trekked through the countryside, they stumbled upon a small group of survivors holed up in an abandoned warehouse.

Ava approached them cautiously, hoping that they would be willing to join forces in the fight against the zombies.

To her relief, the survivors welcomed them with open arms. They introduced themselves as Jayden, Tyler, and Madison.

Jayden was a former military medic with extensive knowledge of medical procedures. Tyler was an engineer who could build anything from scratch. Madison was a former scientist who specialized in genetic engineering.

Together, with their combined skills and knowledge, Ava felt like they might finally have a chance at finding a cure.

They set up a base in the warehouse, taking stock of their supplies and making plans for how best to proceed.

Ava tasked Jayden with setting up a makeshift medical facility where he could begin testing potential cures for Tranq. Tyler worked tirelessly to fortify their defenses and build traps to fend off the zombies.

Madison spent long hours working in the lab, analyzing samples of Tranq and conducting experiments to find a cure.

It was slow progress - they encountered numerous setbacks along the way - but they refused to give up hope. They knew that they were each other's best chance at survival.

Even though they already had tried multiple times before in different states and failed to find a cure.

Missouri

Tranq zombies invade Missouri.Ava and her team raced towards Missouri, knowing that they had to act fast to prevent the virus from spreading any further.

As they drove through the state, they could see the devastation that the Tranq virus had wrought. The streets were littered with abandoned cars and buildings, and packs of zombies roamed the countryside.

For days, they searched for survivors, but it seemed like there was no one left alive. They scoured abandoned research facilities and hospitals, hoping to find clues that could lead them to a cure.

But despite their best efforts, they came up empty-handed. It seemed like the virus had mutated beyond even their wildest expectations, leaving them with no hope of finding a cure.

Ava knew that they couldn't give up. There were still people out there who needed their help - people who were fighting for survival against impossible odds.

With renewed determination, Ava and her team set out into the zombie-infested streets of Missouri once again.

They worked tirelessly day and night, gathering resources and building alliances with other survivors across the state. Slowly but surely, they began to implement their plan to stop the virus from spreading any further.

One by one, they took out the zombie hordes that stood in their way, clearing a path towards a brighter future for all survivors in Missouri.

It was a long and arduous journey, filled with danger and death at every turn. But in the end, Ava's unwavering determination paid off.

They finally found a survivor who claimed to know about a potential cure - a brilliant virologist named Dr. Katherine Shaw.

Some things are just not curable.

Ava's heart sank as she received news of the outbreak in Missouri. It seemed like no matter how hard they tried, the virus was always one step ahead.

But Ava refused to give up. She knew that they had to act fast in order to prevent the virus from spreading any further.

She gathered her team and set out for Missouri, determined to find a way to stop the Tranq zombies once and for all.

As they made their way through the deserted streets of Missouri, Ava couldn't help but feel a sense of deja vu. It was as if they were back in Texas all over again, fighting against an enemy that seemed impossible to defeat.

But this time, Ava had a new weapon in her arsenal - Madison's latest experiment had yielded promising results.

They arrived at the heart of the outbreak, where the Tranq zombies were swarming the streets.

Ava and her team quickly set up a perimeter, using Tyler's traps to keep the zombies at bay while Jayden worked tirelessly to administer Madison's cure to as many survivors as possible.

It wasn't easy - the Tranq zombies were relentless and seemed immune to their usual tactics. But Ava, Jayden, Tyler, and Madison refused to give up.

Days turned into weeks, and slowly but surely, they began to gain ground. The Tranq zombies began to weaken and die off, until finally there were none left.

Ava breathed a sigh of relief as she looked out at the empty streets of Missouri. They had done it - they had finally found a way to stop the Tranq virus from spreading any further.

Kill the zombies. That's the only way to stop the spread.

Ava and her team received a distress signal from a small town in Missouri. They packed up their supplies and set out towards the state, ready to face the new wave of Tranq zombies.

When they arrived, they found the town overrun with the undead. It was worse than any outbreak they had ever encountered before.

But Ava refused to back down. She knew that they had to find a way to fight off the zombies and find a cure for the virus.

They began by quickly setting up a base camp on the outskirts of the town - this time, they were more prepared, with extensive knowledge from their previous experiences.

They made contact with the survivors in the town and began working out a plan to fight back against the Tranq zombies.

Jayden and Madison worked tirelessly in the lab, testing different combinations of chemicals to find a cure for Tranq. Meanwhile, Tyler built traps and fortifications to keep the zombies at bay.

Ava herself led search parties out into the town to gather supplies and rescue any survivors that they could find.

It was a long, grueling battle - but Ava and her team refused to give up. They fought tooth and nail against the zombies, determined to find a way to stop them once and for all.

Finally, after months of research and fighting, Jayden and Madison successfully created a vaccine that could neutralize the effects of Tranq on humans.

Ava couldn't believe it - after all their hard work, they had finally found a cure, or so they stupidly thought.

They administered the vaccine to all of the remaining survivors in Missouri, but it didn't work.

Ava looked out at the world around her as zombies continue wrecking the entire state, and people continue turning into zombies.

Ava and her team had barely gotten their bearings in Missouri when they received word of a new outbreak. Reports indicated that dozens of people had already been infected and turned into Tranq zombies.

Ava didn't hesitate. They packed up their supplies and set out for the affected area, determined to stop the virus from spreading any further.

As they arrived on the outskirts of a small town, they were met with chaos. The streets were overrun with Tranq zombies, and panicked survivors were running in every direction.

Ava immediately took charge, using her experience to lead her team through the hordes of zombies. They fought their way towards the center of town, where the source of the outbreak was believed to be located.

It wasn't long before they discovered a secret laboratory, hidden beneath an abandoned warehouse. Inside, they found a group of scientists who had been working on a new strain of Tranq virus - one that was even more deadly than before.

But these scientists had a different agenda. They wanted to use the virus to create an army of super soldiers. They had been testing the virus on unwitting subjects, turning them into mindless killing machines.

Ava was horrified at what she saw. She knew that if they didn't stop these scientists, the virus would cause even more devastation than before.

With renewed determination, Ava and her team began to fight their way through the maze-like laboratory. They encountered all manner of obstacles, from mutated test subjects to booby traps and security measures.

But Ava refused to give up hope. She knew that they had to find a way to stop this madness once and for all.

Finally, after hours of fighting, they are forced to come to terms with the fact that the state is now in the hands of Tranq zombies and there's nothing they can do to stop them from continuing their reign of terror.

Kansas

Tranq zombies invade Kansas. Ava and her team were on high alert as they received news of the Tranq zombie outbreak in Kansas. They knew that they had to act fast in order to prevent the virus from spreading any further.

As they arrived in the affected area, they found the city already submerged in chaos. Tranq zombies were staggering through the streets, attacking anything and anyone in their path.

Ava and her team quickly set up a perimeter, using all the tricks they had learned from their past experiences. Tyler built traps and fortifications while Jayden and Madison worked tirelessly to find a cure for the virus.

Meanwhile, Ava led search parties out into the city to gather supplies and rescue any survivors that they could find. It was a long, grueling battle, but Ava's team refused to give up.

Days turned into weeks, and gradually, they began to make progress. They managed to rescue more survivors and held off the zombies at bay. But as always, there was a twist.

It became apparent that there was someone behind the outbreak. A mysterious group of people who had engineered Tranq zombies with intent to use them as an army of destruction.

Ava knew that she had to get to the bottom of this, so she sent her team out to gather intelligence while she focused on rescuing and protecting as many survivors as possible.

As their investigation progressed, they discovered that this mysterious group had been experimenting on humans in a secret facility, testing new strains of Tranq virus until they developed one that could create super soldiers out of ordinary people.

Determined to put an end to their madness once and for all, Ava led her team on a mission into the heart of the outbreak.

Ava and her team had just barely escaped Missouri with their lives. As they crossed the border into Kansas, they could see the telltale signs of a new outbreak.

The streets were eerily quiet, but Ava and her team knew better than to let their guard down. They set up camp on the outskirts of a small town, where reports of the virus first surfaced.

They quickly realized that this outbreak was different from any they had encountered before. The Tranq zombies were faster, smarter, and more aggressive than ever before.

Ava and her team were forced to adapt their tactics quickly in order to survive. They used every resource at their disposal - from traps and weapons to Madison's knowledge of virology - to fight off the undead horde.

It was a grueling battle, but Ava refused to give up. She knew that this outbreak posed a threat not only to the people of Kansas but potentially to the entire country.

As they fought off wave after wave of zombies, Ava began to notice something unusual. Some of the zombies seemed different - more intelligent than others.

She soon discovered that the virus had mutated, creating a new strain of Tranq that affected the brain differently. These new zombies were capable of strategic thinking, making them even more dangerous than before.

Ava knew that they had to find a way to stop this new strain of the virus from spreading any further. With Madison's help, they began developing a new vaccine - one that could target the mutated strain directly.

It was a race against time as they worked around the clock in their makeshift lab, but finally, they succeeded. They administered the vaccine to as many survivors as they could, but yet again, it failed.

Ava and her team received horrifying news that Tranq zombies had crossed state lines and were now infecting people all across Kansas. It was a devastating blow, but Ava refused to give up hope.

They quickly made their way to the nearest town, where they found a small group of survivors who were struggling to fend off the endless hordes of Tranq zombies.

Ava knew that they needed to find a way to fight back before it was too late. She rallied her team and the survivors, working tirelessly to come up with a plan.

They spent countless hours fortifying their position, building barricades and traps to keep the zombies at bay. They also scoured the surrounding area for supplies, searching every abandoned building for anything that could be useful.

Despite their best efforts, however, the zombies continued to infest the area, leaving death and destruction in their wake.

Ava knew that they needed to find a way to stop the virus from spreading any further. She had heard rumors of a potential cure located in a nearby research facility, so she set out with her team to investigate.

As they infiltrated the facility, they encountered fierce resistance from security forces who were all too aware of the danger presented by Tranq zombies.

But Ava was determined. She led her team through the facility's twisting corridors and hidden labs until they finally stumbled upon what appeared to be a cure - a massive tank filled with a strange green liquid.

Without hesitation, Ava ordered Madison and Jayden to begin studying the liquid while Tyler stood guard at the door.

It took hours of analysis, but eventually Madison and Jayden discovered that the liquid contained powerful antibodies that could neutralize Tranq, but it's just wishful thinking.

There is no cure. Never has been. Never will be.

Ava and her team had barely recovered from their harrowing experience in Missouri when they received news of another outbreak - this time in Kansas.

They wasted no time in packing up their supplies and heading towards the affected area.

As they arrived on the outskirts of a small town, they were met with a scene of devastation. The streets were littered with the bodies of humans and Tranq zombies alike, and the survivors were few and far between.

Ava knew that they had to act fast. They quickly set up a base camp on the edge of town, and Tyler began to build traps to keep the zombies at bay.

Jayden and Madison worked tirelessly in the lab, attempting to find a cure for the virus before it could spread any further.

Ava herself led search parties out into the town, gathering supplies and rescuing any survivors that they could find. It was a dangerous mission, as the Tranq zombies were everywhere.

But Ava was determined to save as many people as possible. She fought tooth and nail against the zombies, using every trick in her book to stay one step ahead of them.

As days turned into weeks, Ava and her team slowly began to gain ground. They managed to rescue dozens of survivors from the clutches of the Tranq zombies, and Jayden and Madison were making progress in their search for a cure.

But just as things were starting to look up, disaster struck. One of Ava's team members was bitten by a Tranq zombie, and despite all their efforts, he turned into one of them.

Ava was devastated. It seemed like no matter how hard they tried, the virus was always one step ahead.

Mississippi

Tranq zombies invade Mississippi. Ava and her team received news of the outbreak in Mississippi and immediately set out to investigate.

As they arrived in Mississippi, they were met with chaos. The streets were overrun with Tranq zombies, and the surviving humans were struggling to hold them off.

Ava knew that they had to act fast if they wanted any chance of saving the remaining survivors. She rallied her team and began to devise a plan.

They spent hours analyzing the movements of the zombies, trying to find a weakness. And finally, they discovered it.

There was a massive Tranq zombie that seemed to be controlling the others. If they could take it out, they could weaken the rest of the horde.

It was a dangerous mission, but Ava knew that it was their only chance. She led her team into the heart of the city, dodging zombies left and right.

As they closed in on their target, Tyler set up traps to distract the other zombies while Ava and Madison took aim at the massive one.

With a well-placed shot, they took it down, and the other zombies seemed to falter for a moment. It was enough time for Ava and her team to move in and take out as many as possible.

They fought through the streets for what seemed like hours until finally, they managed to clear out most of the zombies. The remaining survivors were safe once again.

Ava knew that their work wasn't done yet. They had to find out who was behind this outbreak and put an end to their madness once and for all.

It took weeks of investigation, but eventually, Ava discovered that a group of rogue scientists had been experimenting with Tranq virus in an abandoned warehouse.

Ava and her team rushed to Mississippi as soon as they received word of the outbreak. They were grimly familiar with the Tranq virus by now, and they knew that every moment counted.

As they entered a small town in Mississippi, they could see the destruction wrought by the zombie army. Buildings lay in ruins, and there was no sign of human life anywhere.

Ava signaled for Tyler to start setting up traps, while Madison and Jayden got to work analyzing the virus. They needed to find a way to stop it before it was too late.

Ava scoured the area, searching for any survivors. She knew that they couldn't fight this battle alone - they needed every able-bodied person they could find.

After hours of searching, Ava finally stumbled upon a group of survivors holed up in an old abandoned church. They were on the verge of starvation, and their spirits were low.

But when Ava arrived, she brought them a glimmer of hope. She explained their plan to take down the Tranq zombies once and for all, and she urged them to join their cause.

The survivors were initially hesitant - they had already lost so much. But Ava's infectious determination and willpower convinced them that there was hope after all.

Together, Ava and her team worked alongside the survivors to fortify their position. They set up barricades and traps, sharing supplies and resources with each other.

Over the next few days, they fought off wave after wave of Tranq zombies. Each time a member of their team fell, Ava felt a sense of loss that was almost unbearable.

But she refused to give up. She knew that their cause was just to keep fighting.

There are no happy endings, except in fairytales and shady massage parlors.

Ava and her team received news of the outbreak in Mississippi while still dealing with the devastation in Kansas. It was a race against time to try and contain the virus before it could spread any further.

They quickly packed up their supplies and made their way towards Mississippi, arriving just in time to see the Tranq zombies begin to overrun the streets.

Ava sprang into action. She set up a base camp on the outskirts of the city, and immediately sent out search parties to gather intel and rescue survivors.

But this outbreak was unlike any they had seen before. The Tranq zombies were even more aggressive and relentless than before, taking down everything in their path.

Ava knew that they needed a new strategy if they were going to stand a chance against this new strain of the virus. She gathered her team together and began brainstorming ideas.

It was Tyler who came up with the solution. He suggested that they try luring the Tranq zombies into a central location, where they could set off explosives and take out as many of them as possible at once.

It was a risky plan, but Ava knew that they didn't have any other options. They set to work immediately, setting up traps and barricades and getting ready for the attack.

When the Tranq zombies came pouring into the central location, Ava's team was ready for them. They set off the explosives, taking out hundreds of zombies in one fell swoop.

The explosion caused chaos throughout the city, but it also gave Ava's team an opportunity to gather survivors and evacuate them to safety.

Over the course of several weeks, Ava's team battled tirelessly against the undead horde.

Ava and her team were exhausted from their previous battles, but they knew they couldn't afford to rest. The Tranq zombies had invaded Mississippi, and the state was in chaos.

They quickly set up a base camp on the outskirts of Jackson, the state capital, and began to assess the situation.

The zombies were everywhere, overwhelming local law enforcement and military forces. Ava knew that they had to act fast if they were going to make a difference.

Using their expertise and experience, Ava and her team launched a coordinated attack on the zombie hordes. They fought with everything they had, using guns, traps, and hand-to-hand combat to take down as many zombies as possible.

The battle was brutal and unforgiving, but Ava refused to give up. She pushed herself and her team harder than ever before, determined to end this latest outbreak once and for all.

As they fought their way through the streets of Jackson, they noticed something unusual. Some of the zombies seemed different - more intelligent than others.

Ava soon realized that the virus had mutated again, creating a new strain that affected the brain even more profoundly. These new zombies were capable of complex thought processes, making them even more dangerous than before.

But Ava wasn't daunted. She knew that they had to find a way to stop this new strain of the virus from spreading any further. With Madison's help, they began experimenting with new vaccines designed specifically for the mutated strain.

It took time and effort, but eventually, they found a formula that worked. They administered the vaccine to as many survivors as possible, hoping that it would be enough to counteract the effects of the virus.

Florida

Tranq zombies invade Florida. Ava and her team were already on high alert when news of the outbreak in Florida reached them. They packed up their gear and began the journey towards the state, prepared for whatever they might face.

When they arrived in Florida, they discovered that the situation was even worse than they had anticipated. The Tranq zombies had overtaken many of the major cities, leaving destruction and devastation in their wake.

Ava and her team knew that they had to act quickly if they were going to save any survivors. They split up into teams, each assigned to different cities across the state.

As they made their way through the streets, they encountered hordes of zombies at every turn. But Ava's team was well-trained and well-equipped, and they managed to take out each wave with ease.

It was while clearing out a hospital in Miami that Ava noticed something strange. One of the Tranq zombies seemed to be more human than the others - almost as if it was trying to communicate with her.

Ava moved closer to the zombie, studying it carefully. As she approached, it suddenly lunged towards her, its eyes burning with an intelligence that she had never seen in a zombie before.

Ava managed to dodge the attack and take down the zombie. But she knew that something was different about this strain of Tranq virus.

She relayed her findings back to Madison, who began conducting tests on the samples that Ava had collected. It didn't take long for them to figure out what was happening.

The Tranq virus had mutated yet again - this time affecting the brain even more profoundly than before. The new strain had created intelligent zombies capable of complex thought processes.

Ava and her team were exhausted from their previous battles, but they knew that they had to keep going. The Tranq zombies had invaded Florida, and the state was in chaos.

They set up a base camp in a small town on the outskirts of Miami, and immediately began to coordinate with local law enforcement and military forces.

But it quickly became apparent that they were outmatched. The Tranq zombies were more aggressive than ever before, and seemed to be multiplying at an alarming rate.

Ava knew that they couldn't afford to wait for backup - they had to act fast if they were going to make a difference.

She organized her team into small squads, each one tasked with clearing out a different area of the city. They worked tirelessly day and night, battling against the undead horde.

But despite their best efforts, the zombies just kept coming. It was like fighting a losing battle - for every zombie they took down, two more seemed to take its place.

It wasn't until they stumbled upon an old research facility in the heart of Miami that they discovered the truth behind the outbreak.

Ava led her team inside the facility, careful to watch out for any traps or surprises. What they found inside was horrifying - a group of scientists had been deliberately infecting people with the Tranq virus, hoping to create an army of undead soldiers.

Ava felt sickened by the sight of it all. She knew that they had to put an end to this madness once and for all.

With Tyler's help, they managed to shut down the facility's power supply, plunging it into darkness. They then set explosive charges throughout the building, hoping to kill off the zombies, but it didn't work.

Ava and her team knew that they had to act fast if they were going to stop the Tranq zombies from spreading further into Florida. They immediately set up a base camp on the coast, near Tampa Bay.

The beaches were littered with wreckage - boats overturned, beach chairs and umbrellas strewn about. It was clear that the Tranq zombies had already caused extensive damage.

As they began to scout the area, Ava's team quickly realized that the population density in Florida would make it much harder to contain the virus.

They knew that they had to come up with a new plan. With Tyler leading the charge, they began using boats to transport survivors out of the infected areas and onto nearby islands.

It wasn't a perfect solution - many of the islands were small and remote, with limited resources. But it was better than nothing.

As they worked tirelessly to gather survivors and get them off the mainland, Ava and her team also continued to fight against the zombie horde.

The Tranq zombies in Florida were especially brutal, their bites causing even more rapid transformations than before. It seemed like every moment counted as they worked to find a cure.

But despite their best efforts, they couldn't keep up with the virus. The outbreak continued to spread, leaving destruction and devastation in its wake.

Ava and her team were forced to retreat back to their base camp, regrouping and seeking a new strategy. They knew that they still had a long way to go before they could finally put an end to this nightmare.

Ava and her team were exhausted from their previous battles, but they knew they couldn't afford to rest. The Tranq zombies had invaded Florida, and the state was in chaos.

They quickly set up a base camp on the outskirts of Miami, the epicenter of the outbreak, and began to assess the situation.

The zombies were everywhere, overwhelming local law enforcement and military forces. Ava knew that they had to act fast if they were going to make a difference.

Using their expertise and experience, Ava and her team launched a coordinated attack on the zombie hordes. They fought with everything they had, using guns, traps, and hand-to-hand combat to take down as many zombies as possible.

The battle was brutal and unforgiving, but Ava refused to give up. She pushed herself and her team harder than ever before, determined to end this latest outbreak once and for all.

As they fought their way through the streets of Miami, they noticed something unusual. Some of the zombies seemed different - more intelligent than others.

Ava soon realized that the virus had mutated again, creating a new strain that affected the brain even more profoundly. These new zombies were capable of complex thought processes, making them even more dangerous than before.

But Ava wasn't daunted. She knew that they had to find a way to stop this new strain of the virus from spreading any further. With Madison's help, they began experimenting with new vaccines designed specifically for the mutated strain.

It took time and effort, but eventually, they found a formula that worked. They administered the vaccine to as many survivors as possible, hoping that it would be enough to counteract the effects of the virus, but it didn't.

Despite their efforts, the virus continued to spread, infecting more and more people. Ava and her team were unsure of what to do next.

As they discussed their options, a group of survivors approached them, led by a man named Jack. Jack had been working on a cure for the Tranq virus, and he believed that he had made a breakthrough.

Ava was skeptical at first, but Jack's research seemed promising. They decided to collaborate with him, pooling their resources and knowledge to create a cure that would work against both the original and mutated strains of the virus.

It was a race against time, but together they worked day and night, testing different combinations of vaccines and treatments until they finally found a solution.

The vaccine was quickly distributed among survivors in the area, and it seemed to be effective. The number of infected began to decrease rapidly, allowing Ava and her team to focus on clearing out the remaining zombies.

As they worked tirelessly to eliminate the undead hordes, Ava couldn't help but feel proud of her team. They had faced some of the toughest challenges imaginable and come out victorious.

With the outbreak finally under control, Ava took a moment to reflect on everything that had happened. She knew that there would always be new threats lurking around every corner, but with her team by her side, she felt confident that they could handle whatever came their way.

For now, she and her team could breathe a little easier, knowing that they had saved countless lives from the deadly Tranq virus.

Ava and her team grew frustrated. They had hoped that the vaccine would work, but it seemed as though the virus was unstoppable.

But then, Tyler had an idea. He suggested that they track down the source of the virus and destroy it once and for all.

Ava knew it was a risky proposition. The scientists responsible for creating the virus were likely well-protected, and going after them could mean certain death.

But she also knew that they had no other choice. They couldn't keep fighting off wave after wave of zombies forever.

With Tyler leading the charge, they began to gather intelligence on the scientists responsible for the outbreak. They scoured records, hacked into databases, and even went undercover to gain more information.

Eventually, they discovered the location of the scientists' secret lab - a remote island off the coast of Florida.

Ava and her team boarded a boat and made their way towards the island, fully prepared to take down anyone who got in their way.

As they approached the island, Ava could feel her heart pounding in her chest. This was it - the moment of truth.

They docked their boat on a rocky outcropping and made their way inland. The island was heavily guarded, with armed soldiers patrolling every corner.

But Ava and her team were well-prepared. They moved quickly and quietly, taking out guards one by one until they reached the heart of the compound.

There, they found the scientists hard at work, developing even more deadly strains of the virus.

Ava saw red. She charged forward, taking down any scientist who got in her way. Her team followed suit, their weapons flashing in the dim light.

As Ava and her team continued to fight against the zombie hordes, they suddenly received a distress call from a nearby research facility. The scientists inside were being held captive by the zombies, and they needed Ava's team to rescue them.

Without hesitation, Ava and her team set out to rescue the scientists. They fought their way through wave after wave of the undead, determined to save as many lives as possible.

When they finally arrived at the research facility, they discovered something shocking. The scientists had been working on a new super-virus that would make the Tranq virus seem like child's play.

Ava knew that they had to stop this new virus from spreading at all costs. She and her team destroyed the research facility and killed all of the infected scientists inside.

But their mission was far from over. They still had to find a way to contain the mutated strain of the Tranq virus before it spread any further.

After much trial and error, Ava and her team developed a vaccine that could effectively stop the mutated strain in its tracks. They administered the vaccine to as many survivors as possible, and slowly but surely, they began to see progress.

The outbreak in Florida was finally under control. The zombie hordes were thinning out, and survivors were beginning to reemerge from their hiding places.

Ava breathed a sigh of relief as she watched the sun rise over Miami. It had been a long, grueling fight, but they had emerged victorious once again.

As she looked out over the deserted streets, Ava knew that this wouldn't be the last time they would face an outbreak of the Tranq virus. But with her team by her side she continued on.

The vaccine's effectiveness was limited, but it did buy them some time. Ava and her team regrouped at their base camp to come up with a new strategy.

They knew that they couldn't just contain the virus - they had to eradicate it entirely. So Ava made a bold decision: she was going to lead her team deep into the heart of the outbreak, to the epicenter of the virus itself.

It would be dangerous, almost suicidal. But Ava knew that it was the only way. She gathered her team together, telling them what needed to be done.

They set out at dawn, moving quickly and quietly through the abandoned streets of Miami. The zombies were everywhere, but Ava and her team were ready for them.

They fought their way through wave after wave of undead, cutting down zombies with expert precision. They moved deeper into the city, following a trail of destruction that led them straight to an old laboratory.

The lab had been abandoned for years, but now it was teeming with zombies. Ava and her team moved cautiously through the building, taking down anything that got in their way.

Finally, they reached the heart of the lab - a room filled with test tubes and equipment. It was here that Ava found what she had been looking for: the source of the virus itself.

She quickly identified the key components of the virus and relayed back to Madison for further analysis. Meanwhile, her team worked to take down every remaining zombie in the lab.

It took hours of fighting and bloodshed, but finally they succeeded in clearing out every last zombie. With one final explosive charge, they destroyed the lab and all remaining traces of the virus.

Eventually even the governor and a former president are turned into Tranq zombies.

Georgia

Tranq zombies invade Georgia. The first to fall to the zombies is a loudmouth transvestite looking female politician who ironically hates transvestites.

As the Tranq zombies spread across Georgia, Ava and her team raced towards the state to stop the outbreak. They arrived just in time to see the chaos unfold.

The streets were littered with abandoned cars and rubble. Zombies roamed freely, attacking anyone in their path. The stench of death hung heavy in the air.

Ava and her team immediately got to work, fighting off zombies and rescuing survivors. They soon discovered that the virus had spread faster than they could have imagined.

The governor and a former president had both been infected and turned into Tranq zombies. It was a shocking blow to morale, but Ava refused to give up.

They continued to fight off the undead, moving from town to town in search of a cure. As they traveled deeper into Georgia, they discovered that the virus had already infected thousands of people.

One day, as they were passing through a small town, they came across a loudmouth transvestite looking female politician who was being attacked by a group of zombies.

Ava and her team quickly intervened, dispatching the zombies with ease. But as they helped the politician to her feet, Ava couldn't help but feel a sense of disgust.

Despite being saved by Ava and her team, the politician immediately began spouting hate speech towards transvestites.

Ava gritted her teeth but kept her cool. She knew that their primary objective was to end the outbreak, not engage in arguments with ignorant politicians.

They continued on towards Atlanta, where they would deliver the cure that would finally put an end to the Tranq virus once and for all.

As they approached the city limits, Ava could feel her heart racing.

As Ava and her team received news of the outbreak in Georgia, they raced to the scene. They knew that this time, things would be even harder than before.

As they arrived in Georgia, they saw the devastation caused by the zombie hordes. The entire city was in chaos, and the streets were filled with the undead.

Ava and her team quickly got to work, taking out zombie after zombie with their weapons. But as they fought their way through the city, something caught their attention.

It was a loudmouth transvestite-looking female politician who was being attacked by a group of zombies. She was screaming for help, but nobody seemed to be coming to her aid.

Ava couldn't help but feel a sense of irony as she watched the woman being devoured by the very same monsters she had likely ridiculed before.

But Ava didn't have time to dwell on it. She knew that there were more pressing matters at hand.

As they continued deeper into the city, Ava and her team began encountering more and more zombies. And soon enough, they ran into some unexpected guests: the governor and a former president who were both turned into Tranq zombies.

Ava knew that this was going to be their toughest fight yet. But she also knew that if they didn't stop these zombies, they would destroy everything in their path.

Ava and her team readied themselves for battle, steeling themselves for what was to come. They charged forward, cutting down zombie after zombie with their weapons.

The battle was long and grueling, with both sides suffering heavy casualties. But finally, Ava and her team emerged victorious.

And then they woke up and realized that they hadn't actually saved anything because they had been dreaming.

As news of the outbreak in Georgia spread, Ava and her team geared up and headed out to the state. They knew that time was of the essence if they were going to contain the virus before it spread too far.

As they made their way through the empty streets of Atlanta, they could see signs of the chaos that had unfolded here. Cars were overturned, buildings were burned out, and there were signs of struggle everywhere.

They soon learned that the first person to fall victim to the Tranq zombies in Georgia was a well-known politician. She had been a vocal opponent of transgender rights and had even advocated for laws that discriminated against the LGBTQ+ community.

Ava couldn't help but feel a sense of irony as she heard this news. But she knew that regardless of the victim's personal beliefs, every life was still worth saving.

They quickly established a base camp in the city and began to gather intelligence on the virus. From what they could tell, it appeared to have originated from an underground laboratory.

Ava led her team into the laboratory, fighting their way through hordes of zombies along the way. Once inside, they discovered that this was no ordinary lab - it had been specifically designed to create biological weapons.

It quickly became clear that whoever had been working in this lab had been experimenting with various viruses and bacteria, trying to create something even deadlier than Tranq.

Ava and her team worked tirelessly to destroy every last trace of these experiments. They destroyed equipment, set fire to samples, and did everything in their power to ensure that these deadly viruses would never be used against humanity again.

The virus can't be contained, or cured.

Ava and her team received the distress call from Georgia and knew they had to act fast. As they made their way towards the state, Ava couldn't help but reflect on how the virus had spread so quickly despite their efforts.

When they arrived in Georgia, they were greeted with chaos. The streets were filled with zombies, and survivors were few and far between.

Ava quickly set up a base camp and began gathering intelligence. They soon learned that the virus had been spread deliberately by a group of extremists who believed that the world needed to be purified.

Ava and her team sprang into action, working to take down the extremist group before they could do any more damage. They fought their way through waves of zombies and finally reached the extremist's headquarters.

There, they found the leader of the group - a loudmouth transvestite looking female politician who ironically hated transvestites.

Ava couldn't believe it. This woman had caused so much destruction and death, all in the name of her twisted ideology.

Without hesitation, Ava charged forward, taking down anyone who got in her way. Her team followed suit, their weapons flashing in the dim light.

They fought their way through the building, finally reaching the room where the politician was hiding. She was surrounded by zombies, using them as a shield against Ava and her team.

But Ava wasn't about to back down. She charged forward, taking down zombie after zombie until she finally reached the politician herself.

The politician snarled at Ava, screaming that she would never back down from her beliefs. But Ava just shook her head in disgust.

"You're nothing but a monster," she said coldly

The Carolinas

Tranq zombies invade South Carolina. Ava and her team received word that the Tranq zombies had spread to South Carolina, and they knew that they had to move fast. They quickly packed up their gear and set out for the state.

As they crossed the state line, they could see the devastation that had been caused by the zombies. Entire towns had been overrun, and there were signs of struggle everywhere.

They quickly set up a base camp and began gathering intelligence on the situation. From what they could tell, the zombies had spread quickly, attacking both large and small communities alike.

Ava knew that they had to act fast if they were going to save anyone in South Carolina. She rallied her team, steeling them for what was sure to be a tough fight.

They began to move through the state, taking out zombies wherever they found them. They soon encountered a group of survivors who were holed up in a small town.

The survivors were scared and desperate for help. They had lost many of their own to the zombie hordes, and they knew that they couldn't hold out much longer.

Ava knew that she couldn't leave these people behind. She ordered her team to fortify the town while she went out on a mission to find any possible leads on how to end the outbreak.

She traveled far and wide, encountering dangerous obstacles along the way. But finally, she found what she was looking for - a laboratory where they were developing an antidote to the Tranq virus.

Ava quickly contacted her team back at the town and instructed them to make their way to the laboratory. They fought their way through hordes of zombies until they finally reached their destination.

Ava and her team received word of the outbreak in South Carolina and immediately set out to contain it. As they entered the state, they could see the devastation caused by the virus.

The streets were filled with zombies, and the survivors were nowhere to be found. As they made their way further into the state, they found a group of survivors who had barricaded themselves in a shopping mall.

The survivors were understandably frightened, but Ava and her team quickly reassured them that they were there to help. Together, they worked to fortify their position and gather supplies.

But as they settled in for the night, Ava couldn't shake off the feeling that something was wrong. She had a nagging feeling that they were being watched.

Sure enough, as night fell, the Tranq zombies attacked the mall. They swarmed in through every entrance, overwhelming Ava and her team's defenses.

The survivors fought bravely alongside them, but there were too many zombies. They quickly realized that their only hope was to escape through an underground tunnel.

Ava and her team led the survivors through the tunnel, fighting off zombies every step of the way. But as they emerged on the other side, they discovered something even more terrifying than the zombies themselves.

There was a cult operating in South Carolina, one that worshiped the Tranq virus as a divine gift sent to purify humanity. They had been responsible for spreading the virus intentionally, believing that only those who believed in their ideology deserved to survive.

Ava knew that they had to stop this cult before it caused any more destruction. They made their way towards the cult's headquarters, a massive compound guarded by heavily armed forces.

Ava and her team received a distress call from South Carolina, where the Tranq zombies had invaded. They knew that they had to act fast before it was too late.

As they crossed the state line, they could see the devastation that had been wrought by the zombies. Buildings were on fire, cars were overturned, and there were signs of struggle everywhere.

Ava led her team into the heart of the city, where they encountered hordes of zombies. They fought their way through the streets, taking out as many zombies as they could.

But no matter how many zombies they killed, there always seemed to be more. Soon enough, it became clear that they were outnumbered and outmatched.

One of Ava's team members was bitten by a zombie and quickly turned into one of them. Ava knew what she had to do - she had to put him down before he hurt anyone else.

With tears in her eyes, Ava raised her weapon and shot her friend in the head. It was a painful reminder of the reality she faced - in this fight against the Tranq virus, there were no winners.

But Ava didn't give up. She and her team continued fighting until they finally reached the source of the outbreak - an underground laboratory that had been conducting experiments on the virus.

Ava knew that they had to destroy the lab before it was too late. They fought their way through waves of zombies until they finally reached the lab.

Inside, they found a group of scientists who had been conducting experiments on innocent people to create more powerful strains of the virus.

Without hesitation, Ava attacked. She fought with all her might, taking down scientist after scientist until she killed them all.

Ava and her team received a distress call from South Carolina: the Tranq zombies had invaded the state. They packed their bags and headed towards the state as quickly as possible, knowing that every second counted.

As they arrived in South Carolina, they could see the devastation caused by the zombie hordes. Buildings were on fire, cars were overturned, and there were signs of struggle everywhere.

Ava knew that they had to act fast if they were going to contain the outbreak. She ordered her team to split up and start taking out as many zombies as possible.

As they fought their way through the streets, Ava couldn't help but feel a sense of dread. They were outnumbered and outmatched, and it seemed like every zombie they took out was replaced by two more.

But Ava refused to give up. She rallied her team, pushing them to keep fighting even when things seemed hopeless.

They made their way towards the city center, where the bulk of the zombie hordes were located. It was a suicide mission, but Ava knew it was their only hope of stopping the outbreak.

The battle was fierce, with both sides suffering heavy losses. But finally, Ava and her team emerged victorious.

They quickly worked to clean up the city, burning zombie corpses and sterilizing contaminated areas. It would take time for South Carolina to recover from the outbreak, but thanks to Ava and her team's efforts, there was still hope for the state's survival.

Tranq zombies invade North Carolina. Ava and her team received news that the Tranq zombies had invaded North Carolina. Despite the exhaustion and trauma from their previous mission in South Carolina, they knew that they had to act fast.

As they crossed the state line, Ava could feel her heart pounding in her chest. She knew that they were walking into a dangerous situation, but she also knew that they were the only ones who could save the people of North Carolina.

The first few days were grueling. They encountered zombie hordes at every turn, and Ava knew that they had to keep moving if they were going to find a way to stop the outbreak.

But as they traveled deeper into the state, Ava began to notice something strange. The zombie behavior seemed more coordinated than usual, almost as if they were being controlled by something.

It wasn't long before Ava and her team discovered the source of this strange behavior - a group of bandits who had created a serum that allowed them to control the Tranq zombies.

These bandits were using the zombies for their own twisted purposes, raiding towns and villages and taking whatever they wanted.

Ava knew that this couldn't go on any longer. She ordered her team to infiltrate the bandit's stronghold and destroy their serum.

It was a dangerous mission, but Ava was determined to see it through. They fought their way through wave after wave of zombie hordes until they finally reached the stronghold.

Inside, they found the bandit leader injecting himself with their serum. Ava attacked without hesitation, taking down every bandit in her path until she reached the leader.

With one swift blow, she knocked the serum out of his hand and destroyed it.

Ava and her team wasted no time in responding to the distress call from North Carolina. They knew that the Tranq virus was highly contagious and that they had to act swiftly to prevent another outbreak.

As they crossed the state line, Ava could see the signs of devastation caused by the zombies. The once peaceful streets were now filled with the undead, and the survivors were nowhere to be found.

Ava led her team towards a small town where survivors had reportedly barricaded themselves in a community center. As they approached, they could hear the desperate cries for help coming from inside.

The survivors had done an admirable job of holding off the zombies, but it was clear that they couldn't hold out much longer. Ava ordered her team to reinforce their defenses while she went out to find any possible leads on how to stop the outbreak.

She searched far and wide, encountering dangerous obstacles along the way. But she remained determined, knowing that there was no time to waste.

Finally, she stumbled upon a group of scientists who had been working on an experimental cure for the Tranq virus. They had managed to develop a serum that would reverse the effects of the virus and restore those infected back to human form.

Ava quickly contacted her team and instructed them to make their way towards the lab. They fought their way through hordes of zombies until they finally reached their destination.

Inside, they found the scientists who had developed the serum. They were relieved to see Ava and her team and quickly handed over vials of the cure.

With vials in hand, Ava and her team made their way back to the community center where the survivors were still fighting for their lives.

Ava and her team received a distress call from North Carolina, where the Tranq zombies had invaded. They knew that they had to act fast before it was too late.

As they crossed the state line, they could see that the virus had spread quickly. The streets were filled with zombies, and the survivors were running out of resources. It was clear that this outbreak was on a much larger scale than the one in South Carolina.

Ava led her team into the heart of the city, where they encountered hordes of zombies. They fought their way through the streets, trying their best to protect any survivors they found.

But no matter how hard they fought, they couldn't seem to contain the outbreak. The zombies seemed to be adapting to their tactics, making them more and more difficult to kill.

One night, as Ava and her team made camp in an abandoned building, they heard strange noises coming from outside. They could hear zombies growling and footsteps approaching.

Suddenly, the door burst open, revealing a group of human survivors armed with guns. They held Ava and her team at gunpoint, accusing them of being responsible for the outbreak.

It turned out that these survivors were part of a doomsday cult that believed the Tranq virus was the end of times. They believed that by embracing the virus, they would be among the chosen few who would ascend to a higher plane of existence.

Ava tried to reason with them, explaining that she and her team were there to help contain the outbreak. But it was no use - the cult members were convinced that Ava and her team were there to stop them from becoming gods.

Ava and her team received news of the Tranq zombie outbreak in North Carolina. They knew they had to act fast if they were going to save anyone.

As they entered the state, they could see that the situation was dire. The streets were filled with zombies, and there were no signs of life anywhere.

Ava led her team towards the nearest settlement, hoping to find survivors in need of their help. But as they arrived, they were met with hostile forces.

A group of survivors had taken control of the settlement and were determined to keep it that way. They fired warning shots at Ava and her team, making it clear that they weren't welcome.

Ava tried reasoning with them, explaining that they were there to help, but the survivors weren't interested. They saw Ava and her team as a threat, and they would do whatever it took to protect their territory.

Undaunted, Ava and her team continued their mission. They worked their way through the state, taking out zombies wherever they found them.

But it soon became clear that the survivors in North Carolina were more hostile than any they had encountered before. They saw outsiders as a threat to their survival and would attack anyone who approached them.

It was a difficult environment for Ava and her team to work in, but they refused to give up. They continued their mission, hoping to find survivors who needed their help.

Finally, after many days of searching, they found a village that had managed to stay safe from the zombie hordes. The village elders welcomed Ava and her team with open arms, grateful for any help they could get.

Together with the villagers, Ava and her team worked to make this place safe.

Colorado

Tranq zombies invade Colorado. The first to be killed by the zombies is the loudmouth idiot of a female politician who was so stupid that she thought she could talk to the zombies, and have them attack her political rivals, but instead the zombies ate her.

As news of the Tranq zombie invasion in Colorado spread, Ava and her team quickly made their way to the state. They were horrified by what they found - the streets were littered with the bodies of both zombies and humans.

But there was one particular body that caught Ava's eyes. The loudmouth idiot of a female politician lay lifeless on the ground, her stomach torn open by the hungry zombies.

Ava had heard about this woman before - she had been trying to use the zombie outbreak for political gain, using it as an excuse to attack her rivals. It was clear that her plan had backfired horribly.

As Ava and her team continued through the city, they encountered small pockets of survivors who were doing their best to stay alive. But it was clear that they needed help if they were going to make it out alive.

With the help of the survivors, Ava and her team came up with a plan to lure the zombies away from the city. They knew that they couldn't defeat them all, but if they could just distract them long enough, the survivors could escape.

The plan worked - as Ava and her team drew the zombies away from the city, the survivors took their chance and fled. It was a close call, but they managed to make it out alive.

As they regrouped outside the city, Ava couldn't help but think about the politician who had met such a gruesome end. She wondered if things would have turned out differently if she had focused on helping people instead of using them for her own gain.

In any case, Ava knew that there was still much work to be done. She and her team continued on their way.

Ava and her team arrived in Colorado to find the streets overrun with Tranq zombies. The chaos was even worse than they had experienced before. The survivors were few and far between, and the zombies had taken control of the city.

As they made their way through the streets, Ava couldn't help but notice the lack of leadership. There was no one in charge, no one trying to rally survivors or take on the zombie threat.

That's when they stumbled upon a small group of survivors who had barricaded themselves in an abandoned warehouse. They were desperate for help, and Ava knew that it was up to her and her team to turn the tide.

They worked tirelessly with the survivors, building barricades and traps to keep the zombies at bay. But as they fought, they couldn't help but wonder why there was such a lack of leadership in this city.

It wasn't until one night, as they sat around a campfire discussing their next move, that they heard a voice shouting from outside. It was a man, standing on a car and waving a gun.

He introduced himself as John, the leader of a small group of survivors who had been working to take out the zombie threat. He explained that they had been fighting for months but that there was no end in sight.

Ava could see that John was passionate about taking on the zombie hordes, but it was clear that he needed help. She offered her team's assistance, hoping that together they could make a real difference.

As they worked with John's group, Ava couldn't help but feel relieved that there was finally someone taking charge. With John's leadership, they were able to push the horde back for now.

Ava and her team arrived in Colorado to find the state already overrun with Tranq zombies. It was a gruesome sight that was all too familiar to them. But what they didn't expect was to come across the dead body of a politician who had been foolish enough to think she could communicate with the zombies.

Despite her gruesome fate, Ava couldn't help but feel a twinge of anger towards the woman. They were already dealing with enough problems without having to deal with politicians who lacked basic common sense.

But there was no time to dwell on that. Ava and her team had a job to do. They fought their way through zombie hordes, trying their best to save as many survivors as possible.

As they made their way deeper into the infected zone, they came across a group of survivors who had barricaded themselves in a shopping mall. They were running low on supplies and were desperate for help.

With no other options, Ava and her team agreed to help them out. They fought their way through hordes of zombies, managing to gather enough supplies to help the survivors hold out a little longer.

But it was clear that they couldn't stay in the mall forever. They needed to find a way out of the state before it was too late.

Ava led her team towards a military base, hoping to find transportation out of the state. Along the way, they encountered more and more zombies, making it clear that the situation had gotten out of hand.

Finally, they arrived at the base only to find it overrun with zombies. It seemed like their hopes of finding transportation were dashed.

But then Ava noticed something strange. There seemed to be a distinct lack of awareness.

Ava and her team received the news of the Tranq zombies invading Colorado. As they arrived, they could see that the situation was grim. The streets were filled with the undead, devouring everything in sight.

As they made their way towards the Capitol building, where the governor had set up their base of operations, Ava noticed a commotion in the distance. A group of survivors were trying to fight off a horde of zombies, but they were vastly outnumbered.

Ava ordered her team to split up and help the survivors while she went ahead to meet with the governor. She knew that time was of the essence and that they needed to come up with a plan fast if they were going to save Colorado.

As Ava entered the Capitol building, she could hear panicked voices coming from the Governor's office. She burst through the door to find the Governor huddled in a corner, surrounded by his advisors.

"Governor, what's going on?" Ava demanded.

The Governor looked up at her with fear in his eyes. "It's chaos out there," he said. "The zombies came out of nowhere and started attacking everyone. We don't know what to do."

Ava looked at him coldly. "Well, we do," she said. "We're going to take back this city block by block until it's safe again."

With that, Ava rallied her team and set out into the streets once again. They fought their way through hordes of zombies, taking back territory one block at a time.

As they worked their way towards the center of town, they encountered a group of survivors who had barricaded themselves in a high-rise.

The Dakotas

Tranq zombies invade South Dakota.

As Ava and her team made their way through the streets, they couldn't help but notice people setting up refuge camps. They were clearly leaving the city - instead of dealing with the problem head on, they were all running away.

Ava knew that she had to convince the Governor to take action. She raced back towards the Capitol building and burst through the door of the Governor's office once again.

"Governor," she said sternly, "this stop-and-start approach is not working. You need to get people back into the streets and fight or we're going to lose this war!"

The Governor looked at her with cold eyes, knowing that she was right. But with so many people running from the city, he didn't see how it could be done. He and his advisors huddled together in a corner, trying to come up with a plan.

Ava left the office for a moment to confer with her team, figuring they'd be better at coming up with a strategy than everyone else in that room. As they talked over ideas amongst themselves, they could hear muffled voices coming from inside the Governor's office once again.

Ava burst back into the room as soon as she heard them shouting. The Governor was pounding his fist on the table while his advisors talked non-stop at him.

Ava strode towards them quickly, causing them to quiet down immediately.

"With all due respect," she said sharply to the Governor.

Thanks to a tip from a survivor, Ava and her team arrived in the southern part of South Dakota to find the streets overrun with Tranq zombies.

Ava couldn't help but think about all the survivors. The Tranq zombies were highly dangerous and unpredictable, and it was clear that anyone still living here would be in serious danger without the help of her team.

In order to survive the undead threat, everyone would have to work together to keep each other safe - an ideal Ava believed in very strongly.

Ava knew that she had to stop the source of the invasion or else they would be fighting this plague for months on end. But as she looked around, she realized that there wasn't a single zombie in sight - how could that be?

Just then, Ava heard a voice cry out from behind some nearby crates. "Hey!" one of the survivors shouted. "Over here!"

Ava worked quickly to clear a path to the survivor, then asked what had happened. "We were s-supposed to meet up with representatives from CDC today," one of the shaken survivors said between sobs. "The government said that they wanted to help us fight off these zombies."

Ava gazed at them for a moment before turning around and letting out a low curse. It looked like the government had lied again - she knew that whenever people thought big government was going to save them, you could expect only more trouble.

Ava turned to face her team and knew what she needed to do.

Capital of Abraham

Ava and her team arrived in South Dakota to find the streets overrun by Tranq Zombies. It was a gruesome sight that was all too familiar. But what they didn't expect was to come across the dead body of a politician who had been foolish enough to think she could communicate with the zombies.

Despite her gruesome fate, Ava couldn't help but feel a twinge of anger towards the woman. They were already dealing with enough problems without having to deal with politicians who lacked basic common sense.

But there was no time to dwell on that. Ava and her team had a job to do. They fought their way through zombie hordes, trying their best to save as many survivors as possible.

As they made their way deeper into the infected zone, they came across a group of survivors who had barricaded themselves in an abandoned warehouse. They were running low on supplies and were desperate for help.

With no other options, Ava and her team agreed to help them out. They fought their way through hordes of zombies, managing to gather enough supplies to help the survivors hold out a little longer.

But it was clear that they couldn't stay in the warehouse forever. They needed to find a way out of the state before it was too late.

Ava led her team towards a military base, hoping to find transportation out of the state. Along the way, they encountered more and more zombies, making it clear that the situation had gotten out of hand.

Finally, they arrived at the base only to find it overrun with zombies.

Tranq zombies invade North Dakota. Ava and her team retreated back to the city, not yet ready to give up on finding a way out of the state. They continued to fight their way through the infected streets, determined to help as many survivors as possible along the way.

As they made their way through North Dakota, Ava heard rumors of a supposed safe zone in the capital city of Abraham. It was their last hope - if it turned out to be true, then they might finally find a way out of this nightmare.

But when they arrived in Abraham, they found only more chaos. The streets were empty and silent, and there wasn't a single survivor in sight.

Ava knew that they had come too far to give up now. She and her team began searching every building, determined to find any clue that might lead them to safety.

After hours of searching, Ava finally stumbled upon what appeared to be a secret underground bunker. It was locked tight, but Ava knew that they had no other choice. Her team worked furiously to break through the doors while Ava stood watch outside.

Finally, they broke through the final layer of security and rushed inside. To their relief, they found survivors huddled together inside - people who had been smart enough to seek shelter before the outbreak hit.

Ava felt a weight lift off her shoulders as she realized that they might finally be safe. But as she looked around at the faces of the survivors, she couldn't help but feel an overwhelming sense of responsibility. The zombies weren't going away anytime soon, and it was up to her and her team to make sure that these people had a chance at survival.

With renewed determination, Ava vowed to find a way to get all of the survivors to a place where the zombies can't get to them.

Ava and her team were exhausted, but they knew they had to keep fighting. The Tranq zombies were spreading like wildfire, and if they didn't act fast, the entire country would be infected.

They had managed to get some survivors out of South Dakota, but they needed to move quickly if they hoped to save more. They set out towards North Dakota, hoping to intercept the zombies before they could spread even further.

As they made their way through the state, they encountered a group of survivors who had barricaded themselves in a small church. They were running low on supplies and were desperate for help.

Ava and her team agreed to assist them, knowing that every survivor counted in this fight. They fought their way through hordes of zombies, gathering supplies and ammunition along the way.

But as they neared the end of the street, they encountered a new type of zombie - faster and more deadly than anything they had seen before. The survivors called them "sprinters", and Ava realized that these new zombies posed an even greater threat than the Tranq variety.

She turned to her team and gave them a grim look. They would have to adapt quickly if they wanted to survive this battle. Ava knew that there was no time to waste - they needed to plan fast if they were going to save North Dakota.

Ava and her team had just finished their mission in South Dakota, but news of the Tranq zombie invasion in North Dakota had reached them. They were tired, but they knew they had to act fast. Ava gathered her team and headed towards North Dakota, determined to stop the zombie invasion.

As they made their way towards the heart of the outbreak, Ava couldn't help but feel a sense of dread. The Tranq zombies were even more dangerous than regular zombies, and it was clear that this would be their toughest mission yet.

As they entered the city, they saw firsthand the devastation caused by the zombie plague. The streets were littered with corpses, and the sound of moaning zombies echoed through the empty buildings.

But Ava and her team were not deterred. They fought their way through the zombie hordes, taking out as many as they could. As they got closer to the epicenter of the outbreak, they encountered more powerful Tranq zombies who were harder to take down.

But Ava was a master strategist. She knew how to take down even the most powerful zombies. With her team at her back, she led them straight into the heart of the outbreak.

And when they finally arrived at the source of the invasion—a government facility—the truth about what had happened came to light. The government had been experimenting with a new drug that was supposed to turn violent criminals into docile citizens. But something had gone terribly wrong, and instead of creating docile citizens, it had created an army of Tranq zombies.

Ava and her team knew what had to be done. They fought their way into the facility, taking out any zombies that stood in their way.

Ava knew that they had to act fast if they were going to save North Dakota. She rallied her team and they made their way towards the center of the state, fighting off zombies as they went.

As they approached the city of Bismarck, they could see that it had already been overrun by Tranq zombies. The streets were littered with debris and the sound of moaning filled the air.

Ava knew that they had to find a way into the city if they were going to save any survivors. They made their way towards the outskirts of the city, hoping to find a way in undetected.

It wasn't long before they came across a group of survivors who had barricaded themselves in a school building. They were running low on supplies and were on the brink of giving up.

Ava and her team agreed to help them out, fighting off zombies as they gathered supplies for the survivors. It was a difficult task, but they managed to get what was needed and brought it back to the school.

After ensuring that everyone was safe, Ava turned her attention back to saving the rest of the state. She knew that she had to come up with a plan fast if they were going to succeed.

She called her team together and together they came up with a plan to lure the zombies away from the city. It was risky, but it was their only hope.

They headed towards an area of dense forest near the Canadian border, using loudspeakers to attract as many zombies as possible. Once they had enough, Ava ordered her team to set fire to the forest.

The plan worked better than expected - as soon as the zombies heard the noise they went towards the fire, but quickly realized that it was a trap and turned around.

Arizona

Tranq zombies invade Arizona. The first to be killed is the idiot make believe governor who tries yell at the zombies for killing the former president who she worships.

Ava and her team arrived in Arizona just in time to see the Tranq zombies invading the city. They could hear screams of terror coming from every direction, and Ava knew that they had to act fast if they wanted to save anyone.

She looked around at her team, determination etched into their faces. This was going to be a tough mission, but she had faith in them.

As they made their way through the city, fighting off zombies as they went, they came across a group of survivors hiding in a nearby diner. They were terrified and barely holding on, but Ava wouldn't let them give up.

She rallied them and gave them hope, telling them that they would make it out alive. And with that, they set out to find a way out of the city.

But as they moved towards the outskirts of town, they encountered the idiot governor who was trying to yell at the zombies for killing the former president she worshipped. Ava shook her head - this wasn't the time for politics.

But before she could do or say anything, the governor was attacked by a group of Tranq zombies. Ava quickly stepped in to save her, fighting off the zombies with everything she had.

As they continued through the city, Ava realized that this wasn't just an ordinary Tranq zombie invasion. There was something different about these zombies - they were stronger, faster and more intelligent than any zombie she had seen before.

She knew that they would have to adapt quickly if they wanted to survive this fight. With her team at her back, she led them deeper into the heart of the outbreak.

Ava and her team received word that Arizona had been overrun with Tranq zombies, and that the governor had been killed. Ava couldn't help but feel a sense of satisfaction at hearing the news - she had never been fond of the governor, who seemed more concerned with image than actual governance.

But Ava knew that she couldn't let her personal feelings get in the way of saving lives. She and her team set out towards Arizona, determined to stop the zombie invasion and save as many survivors as possible.

As they entered the state, they saw the devastation caused by the Tranq zombies. The streets were littered with corpses, and the sound of moaning echoed through the empty buildings.

Ava and her team quickly got to work, fighting their way through hordes of zombies. They encountered some resistance from a group of survivors who had barricaded themselves in a mall, but Ava was able to reason with them and convince them to let her team help.

Together they fought off wave after wave of zombies, gathering supplies and ammunition as they went. But just as they thought they had gained a foothold, they ran into a new type of zombie - one that appeared to be immune to Tranq antidotes.

Ava quickly realized that these zombies were different from any they had ever encountered before. They were extremely fast and agile, and seemed to be able to think on their feet.

Ava knew that they needed to come up with a new strategy if they were going to survive this battle. She called her team together and together they brainstormed ideas.

Finally, Ava came up with a plan. They would lure the zombies away from the city and into an open area.

Ava and her team arrived in Arizona just as the Tranq zombie invasion was in full swing. As they made their way towards the city, they could see that the situation was worse than they had imagined.

The streets were filled with zombies, and the few survivors who remained were fighting a losing battle. They had managed to hold off the Tranq zombies for a while, but it was clear that they couldn't keep it up forever.

Ava and her team knew that they had to act fast if they were going to save anyone. They fought their way through the zombie hordes, taking out as many as they could.

As they approached the governor's mansion, they could hear the sound of yelling coming from inside. When they entered, they found the governor screaming at the zombies, blaming them for killing the former president who she worshipped.

Ava couldn't believe what she was seeing. The governor was completely delusional, and it was clear that she had lost touch with reality.

But there was no time to waste - they had to get out of there before the zombies broke down the doors. Ava quickly rallied her team and led them back outside.

As they made their way towards a safe zone, Ava couldn't help but wonder how many other survivors were being led by delusional leaders like the governor. It was clear that this plague had brought out the worst in people, and it was up to Ava and her team to make sure that those who remained had a chance at survival.

They fought for hours, taking out wave after wave of Tranq zombies. But no matter how many they killed, it seemed like there were always more.

Ava and her team had been sent to Arizona to take care of a Tranq zombie invasion, and they had been making good progress. However, things took an unexpected turn when they encountered the governor, who had foolishly tried to confront the zombies.

Ava watched as the governor was quickly devoured by the Tranq zombies, her screams filling the air. It was clear that her death was a result of her own stupidity and arrogance.

Ava quickly took charge, ordering her team to secure the area and gather as much information as possible about the source of the outbreak. It wasn't long before they discovered that a rogue scientist had been experimenting on prisoners with the Tranq drug, resulting in the zombie invasion.

Ava knew what had to be done - they had to find the scientist and stop him before it was too late. With renewed determination, she led her team towards the scientist's secret laboratory.

As they entered the lab, they were confronted by hordes of Tranq zombies. But Ava and her team were well-prepared - they took out each zombie with precision and efficiency.

Finally, they made their way to the heart of the lab, where they found the scientist. He was seething with anger, but there was a hint of fear in his eyes when he saw Ava and her team.

Without hesitation, Ava charged towards the scientist, taking him down with a single punch. As she stood over his motionless body, she couldn't help but feel a sense of relief - they had succeeded in stopping the outbreak before it could spread any further.

With their mission complete, Ava and her team left Arizona, satisfied that they had saved countless lives.

There are no happy endings.

The Country Has Fallen

City by city. State by state. No matter how hard they try no one can stop the Tranq zombies and soon the zombies have overrun the entire country.

There is no hope. The country has fallen to the zombies.Ava and her team fought valiantly, but in the end, it was all for naught. The

Tranq zombies proved too strong, too fast, too numerous. They swept through the land like a tidal wave, leaving nothing but destruction and death in their wake.

Ava knew that there was no way to survive against the horde. She had seen the devastation firsthand, and she knew that it was only a matter of time before they were overrun.

She had lost many friends and colleagues along the way - brave men and women who had fought to the bitter end. But no matter how hard they tried, they could not hold back the tide of zombies.

In the end, Ava and her team were forced to retreat into an abandoned building. They fortified their position as best they could, but they knew that it was only a matter of time before the zombies found them.

They waited in silence for hours, expecting the worst. But when the zombies finally broke down their defenses, Ava and her team were ready.

They fought with everything they had - guns, knives, fists - but it was no use. The zombies overwhelmed them with sheer numbers, tearing them apart limb by limb.

Ava fought until her last breath, knowing that she had done everything she could to try and save her country. But as she breathed her last breaths, she knew that it was all in vain.

The country had fallen to the Tranq zombies. The world as we knew it was gone forever. All that remained were a few pockets of survivors struggling to eke out an existence in a world overrun by zombies.

And yet even in this darkest of times.

Ava stands atop a high-rise building, gazing out at the sea of Tranq zombies below. She has fought tirelessly to save as many survivors as she could, but now she knows that it is pointless.

There is no one left to save. The zombies have won.

Ava takes one last look at the city before turning to leave. She walks down the stairs of the building, moving past row after row of the undead.

For a moment, Ava pauses and looks at the shambling horde before her. Even in death, they continue to move forward, driven by an insatiable hunger for flesh.

But it's not just the zombies that Ava mourns - it's the loss of humanity. The country has fallen, and with it has fallen all hope for a better future.

As Ava continues her journey through the zombie-infested wasteland, she can't help but wonder if there are any other survivors out there. But even if there are, what hope is there for a world ruled by the dead?

Despite everything she has seen and experienced, Ava refuses to give up hope. She knows that there must be a way to defeat this unnatural plague of death.

But until that day comes, she will fight on. Not for herself, but for every person who was lost in the chaos and destruction of the endless zombie horde.

The country may have fallen, but Ava will never surrender.

Ava watched as the last of her team fell to the hordes of Tranq zombies. Their screams echoed through the streets, but there was no one left to hear them.

She knew that she was the last survivor - the last hope for humanity. But as she looked out at the sea of zombies that surrounded her, she couldn't help but think that it was hopeless.

There were just too many of them. And they were too strong. Ava had fought in countless battles, but she had never seen anything like this.

She knew that this was the end. The country had fallen to the zombies, and there was nothing anyone could do to stop them.

In a moment of desperation, Ava pulled out her gun and aimed it at her head. She closed her eyes and took a deep breath, preparing for the final act.

But before she could pull the trigger, she heard a faint sound coming from the distance. At first, Ava thought it was just another wave of zombies, but as the sound grew louder, she realized that it was something else entirely.

Ava watched in awe as a group of survivors emerged from the horizon. They were heavily armed and ready for battle.

Ava couldn't believe what she was seeing - there were still people out there fighting against the zombies. Maybe there was still hope after all.

With renewed determination, Ava joined forces with the survivors and led them into battle against the horde of Tranq zombies.

They fought tirelessly day and night, pushing back against the relentless tide of zombies. But no matter how many they killed, it seemed like there were always more waiting to take their place.

As days turned into weeks and weeks turned months, then years, all hope was lost.

Ava couldn't believe what she was seeing. The country she had sworn to protect was now nothing more than a wasteland of death and destruction.

Despite her best efforts, the Tranq zombie invasion had proven too much for her and her team. They had fought tirelessly, taking out as many zombies as they could, but in the end, it had all been for nothing.

Ava knew that there was no going back now. The world she had known was gone forever, and there was no way to bring it back.

But even in the midst of all this chaos and destruction, Ava refused to give up hope. She knew that there were still survivors out there, struggling to survive in this new world.

She and her team set out on a new mission - to find those who remained and offer them whatever aid they could. They traveled from city to city, searching for any sign of life.

It wasn't long before they encountered a group of survivors holed up in a military base. The survivors were led by a tough-as-nails commander named Jack, who was initially skeptical of Ava and her team.

But as they worked together to fight off a massive horde of zombies, Jack began to see that Ava and her team were their only hope for survival.

Over the next several months, Ava and her team worked alongside Jack and his group, doing everything they could to keep the zombies at bay. They fortified the base, scavenged for supplies, and trained the survivors in combat techniques.

Despite their best efforts, however, they knew that they couldn't hold out forever. The zombies just kept coming, wave after wave.

In the end, everyone dies.

The End

Also by Aaron Abilene

Carnival Game
Shades of Z

Standalone
The Victims of Pinocchio
A Christmas Nightmare
Pain
Tranq

Ingram Content Group UK Ltd.
Milton Keynes UK
UKHW040811200723
425492UK00001B/68